'NADA

by
DANIEL BOYD

MONTAG

First Montag Press E-Book and Paperback Original Edition April 2023
Copyright © 2023 by Daniel Boyd

As the writer and creator of this story, Daniel Boyd asserts the right to be identified as the author of this book.

Montag Press ISBN: 978-1-957010-25-0
Design © 2023 Amit Dey

Montag Press Team:

Cover Illustration - Ana Sanchez
Cover Design - Rick Febre
Editor - Charlie Franco
Managing Director - Charlie Franco

A Montag Press Book
www.montagpress.com
Montag Press
777 Morton Street, Unit B
San Francisco CA 94129 USA

Montag Press, the burning book with the hatchet cover, the skewed word mark and the portrayal of the long-suffering fireman mascot are trademarks of Montag Press.

Printed & Digitally Originated in the United States of America
10 9 8 7 6 5 4 3 2 1

This book is a work of fiction. Names, characters, places, and incidents are either products of the author's vivid and sometimes disturbing imagination or are used fictitiously without any regards with possible parallel realities. Any resemblance to actual persons, living or dead, events, or locales is entirely coincidental.

For Dad

CHAPTER 1

WHEN I FIRST MET RAY he was on the run from the Mexican Police.

I didn't know that right away, of course. Right away he was just a man handy with a Winchester at a place and time where we needed a useful hand and a long gun. And at that, he was more the Dutchman's hired man than any friend of mine. I didn't get to know him till later. Didn't really like him much at first. And now I come to think on it, I guess I only knew him just a week before we parted company like we did.

Funny how that worked out.

That particular place and time was a played-out mine called Old Pesos—deserted except for me, and I was pretty well played-out myself—along the edge of the Great Salad Desert, northern Mexico, 1936. Back in the States, it was what they called the Great Depression; good times had been over and done with quite a ways back by then and didn't look to be coming round again any time soon. Franklin Roosevelt had got to be president, and he said there was nothing to be afraid of, but now and then I'd catch an American newspaper, and nothing in it but bankrupts, breadlines, and no bottom in sight. Bad news wasn't even news by then.

Down in Mexico, it was worse.

Folks down here never had much to start with, and if they got a little ahead, some fat land-owner generally took most of it. Or some *bandito*, which amounted to the same thing. Or some liberator, which was a sight worse, since the *Federales* might take a notion to shoot you for letting yourself get robbed by a Revolutionary. And that was back in good times.

Now, hard times were here. Land-owners were squeezing blood out of the *peons*, and the *banditos* sucked up whatever was left. Of course, by '36 the revolutions had pretty much dried up and blown away, but that didn't help any—there wasn't much government up there to overthrow anyway.

Not that I was much concerned with Mexicans' troubles right then; had plenty all my own, thank you, stuck there at Old Pesos Mine.

That morning when it all started, I was rousing up in the shack I called my office, which doubled as my living quarters, there in the desert at dawn's early light. I finished making up the cot and swept the dust out, and decided before breakfast I'd re-read the last letter come my way to date. It was from Biegel & Biegel, the folks who took over the place when old man Kurtz went bust, and it said, "Just stay down there and keep an eye on things, we'll find us a buyer and get you paid next month."

It was dated last year. Early last year.

Yeah, and Christ was coming back too, any day now, but no sense setting a place at the table tonight. I was thinking it was getting close to closing time at Old Pesos, and I'd best pull up stakes if I had any, and get myself back home. Would have been nice to get my car back first—it was just a Maxwell, but it always run good—but as that didn't seem likely...

Then, in the light of that new-come morning, I looked up from the Biegel boys' letter, out the hole-in-the-wall I called a window, and saw a cloud of dust, way-aways in the distance. There weren't many cars in that part of Mexico those days, and I thought at first it must be the Serrano brothers, and maybe this was my chance to get my Maxwell back.

Turned out I was wrong, but not by much.

That dust cloud took the better part of a half-hour to get from the horizon to Old Pesos, moving along the spur road that runs down from the government highway. That was time enough for me to holster up the Harrington and take a look through the war-surplus telescope. What I saw was an old U.S. Army ambulance, faded dirt brown, sun-bleached and heavy-loaded from the look of it, beating down the road maybe 35 mph, which is going some on a road like that, and I wondered what was the hurry till it got close—and I saw another cloud of dust just topping the horizon back the way it'd come, maybe fifteen minutes or so behind it. That second dust cloud was beating Hell headed this way, too.

"Guess we got company," I said to nobody at all. Then I slid the holster over to my left side so's I could get a quick cross-draw if one was needed, and I walked down from the Office Shack to the fence. Yeah, there was this fence, right out there at the edge of the desert.

Back when I got there, Old Pesos Mine was just empty holes in a cliff, big piles of rock, a few shacks, and some old machinery that wasn't worth moving. The whole mess was spread over a gentle slope of gravel maybe a half-mile long and a half-mile wide, with a packed-down path of thick yellow clay for the trucks to get up and down, and a drainage channel alongside the clay path where the water from the mine flowed down to a bigger ditch across the front. There on the edge of the desert, there was a pretty good aquifer, which is good because you can't run a mine without water and lots of it.

Anyway, that ditch across the front of the whole works was maybe ten foot deep, ten foot wide, and it run the whole length of the place, like a moat almost, with a wood bridge across it to get out to the spur road that led to the Highway. I guess back in the old days it was dug for protection from Indians, and it worked well enough, probably, but back when he thought Old Pesos was going to make him some money—and back when he was still paying me—old man Kurtz wrote me to put up a fence. I wrote him there wasn't much point in it because no one was going to get away with anything out here in all this empty without a really big truck, and he wrote me to put up the damn fence anyway. So I got hold of some war-surplus concertina wire and strung it across the front, alongside the ditch.

That was the fence, and I always thought it a damn-fool thing, but maybe it saved my life that day.

But that came later. Just then I was walking down to the wood bridge, with the friendly weight of the Harrington in a big leather flap-holster on my left hip as the truck rolled up and stopped on the far side.

The man who got out first was young, in his twenties maybe, with sandy hair falling over one blue eye, and shiny sunburned cheeks glittering with a two-day growth of blonde stubble. He got down stiffly, shaking dust off his khaki shirt.

"I'm beg the pardon, sir," his bad Spanish had a strong accent: German maybe, but not quite. "Can you say we are far from Guanajuato?" He looked back at the cloud of dust coming from whoever was following him, then at me.

Just then another guy got down from the far side of the truck. He was a dark Mexican, maybe the same age as the other man, but rougher: smaller than me but better-muscled, with skin like polished redwood, high cheek-bones, and coarse black hair. The stubble on his face was meaner-looking and there was a funny twist to his mouth. He didn't look at me, or back the way they'd come, just stretched his arms and legs like there wasn't another care in the world.

This one will bear watching, I said to myself, but to sandy-hair, I said in Spanish, "You're not far, but you took the wrong road. You'll have to go back to the main highway. Back the way you came."

His eyes widened just for a second. Then he made himself calm—I could see the effort—and he asked, "There is another way? Back to the Highway? To Guanajuato?"

"I fear there is not," In Spanish, the words were patient and polite. "This road is a spur from the Highway to this mine. There is but one way in, and the same way out."

The nervous look ran off him and he just looked tired. He shot a hang-dog look back at the dust-cloud coming up the spur road in our direction, then turned back to me.

"I fear we must ask you favor," he said it like he was asking for two lumps in his tea, "There are bandits follow us. They had tried stop us on the road a few times ago. I believe that is how we happen to come upon this way—."

Just then the other guy cut in, talking English as good as mine, "You speak Dutch, Mister?"

"Sorry no," I answered back in English, "I got a little French, and Mexican of course, but that's all."

"No good," he shook his head, "*Mijnheer* Ryckman's English is worse even than his Spanish—" He switched back to Spanish and finished "—He's trying to say there's a car full of cut-throats headed here, and they're sort of upset with us."

"There's a car full of something," I talked slow-Spanish for the Dutchman's sake and looked back at the growing dust-cloud coming up the spur road. "But we have maybe some minutes until they get here."

"If you wish to avoid trouble, we will leave, *Senor*," the sandy-haired fellow—Ryckman, I guess his name was—said, "But if you or some of your men wish to assist us, we-we ..." I could see him figuring in his head. "... We will pay to fifty dollars each man for the services."

"It is unfortunate," I said, "But there are no other men at this place. Only I alone."

He sighed and looked back the way they came. "We should perhaps leave, then."

"I should advise not," I said. "There is no road beyond here for your truck. Only rocks and the sun. How many pursue you?"

Ryckman hesitated. The other guy said, "As many as a car will carry. Six perhaps. In an old and noisy car."

"It wasn't noisy when they got it," I said in English, "Is one of them a fat dirty-looking bastard named Serrano?"

The dark guy smiled—a real ugly smile. "We had no time to exchange names ..." The twist in his face got deeper, and I saw now it wasn't a smile, but an old and nasty scar up-side his mouth. "... And I know nothing of his parents. But he carries much belly, and an ass to match."

"That would be Paco Serrano," I nodded, "And that would be my car he's driving: stole it from me a month back." Then back to Spanish, "This is no doubt the best place to stand against him if you intend to stand against him." I pointed to the cliff behind me, "Best to put the truck out of sight; it will fit in any of those tunnels, but the third one—under the overhang—is best. Go slowly and you'll raise no dust."

The dark guy jumped back in the truck and started gently across the bridge and up the slope. But not before

Ryckman pulled out a bolt-action carbine and a box of shells. "Do you require weapon?" He asked me.

"I have weapon," I slapped my holster. "But perhaps we should move some of these crates to block the bridge." Back in the days when Kurtz thought he could make Old Pesos a going concern, he shipped in all kinds of supplies, and I kept the wooden crates they came in stacked down near the fence, always meaning to do something with them someday. They were big but easy to move, and they looked solid enough to stop a car coming over that bridge. "By the way," I said, "My name's Culley. Vernon Culley."

"I am called Janse Ryckman."

We were hauling crates onto the bridge, so we didn't actually shake hands, but something in his manner—or maybe just his bad Spanish—was formal and friendly like that.

"I am of Amsterdam, a merchant."

"I am of Kansas City," I said, "A mining engineer," and while we forted up crates on our side of the bridge, I told him a little bit about how I came to be there. It seemed to reassure him.

"I am to deliver ... cargo to buyer in Guanajuato," he said, "But there are many troubles. The other man, the one who drives, it is his truck and he helps me. He is called Ray."

That's the dark-haired man with the scar, and that's the only name I ever knew him by. He could have been Ramon or Raiford, or Rasputin, for all I know; the Dutchman never told me and I never thought to ask.

"When I deliver it cargo, I have then money to reward your help," Ryckman said, "The money will be good and I shall return to my wife who awaits me in Laredo City. But first—" he turned his carbine toward the bridge and worked a round into the chamber, "I suppose we must attend to these."

CHAPTER 2

*T*hese was pulling up to the bridge as he spoke. Close enough that I saw for sure it was my car—no mistaking the look of that old Maxwell—and Paco Serrano was driving. Never cared much for Paco, but I was glad to see the car again, even if it did look kind of sorry. For a minute I thought it was about to look sorrier because Serrano was going to head it straight into the stack of crates on the bridge, which would be a damn shame for the Maxwell, but he pulled up on the far side at the last second and got out—him and about six other guys—and looked across the bridge at us with his big, sad eyes.

I should tell about Paco's boys now, or else you might picture they looked like *banditos* you see in the movies: Nothing like it. Paco Serrano had read all about Al Capone in the papers, and he and his brothers, Tony and 'Cento, they styled themselves like sure-enough Chicago Hoods. Their boys did too, and it used to be they looked kind of slick, in expensive suits, white shirts, and shiny derbies. Now, though, the hats were dingy, the suits frayed, and the white shirts a yellow-gray memory. And the men that wore them looked sullen and hungry.

See the Serrano brothers started as bandits—and ended up that way, too, just a week from now—but a few years back, they moved up a notch or two in the Social Register and made their way as pretty successful bootleggers—*contrabanderos*. Tony did the fancy shooting, 'Cento was the Muscle, and sad-faced Paco supplied whatever brains they needed. Which wasn't much. But Paco was a born leader, his skinny brother Tony had a way with a gun, and their one-eyed brother 'Cento... well 'Cento was even fatter than Paco, and big—I mean Big—with one bad eye (Which he got from getting on Paco's nerves once too often, somebody told me.) and he was strong like only a really fat man can be. They say 'Cento once strangled somebody's goat with just one hand, and he looked like he could do it too.

So I guess back in the '20s, the Serrano brothers made a pretty slick team, hauling hooch between Saltillo and Monterrey where they sold it to their business partners up North, and the story goes they did a gaudy job of making sure nobody competed with them too much. Paco Serrano had a head for the business, and in fact when I first come to Old Pesos and told him about Kurtz's plans to haul silver out of it again, he looked at me as a potential source of customers and transportation. I guess he had visions of men and trucks streaming in and out of this hole in the desert, and he used to invite himself over for dinner now and again—there's a fair-sized bunk-house at Old Pesos that used to be the mess hall too—keeping an eye on the equipment and supplies coming in, and calculating, I guess, the potential for long-term profit. Sometimes he'd even bring some rum or tequila for the dinner.

Then, like I said, Hard Times came, and Old Pesos wasn't much of a potential customer anymore —not that the Serrano boys had anything to sell these days; when the bottom fell out of just about everything and the bootlegging trade dried up, they had to pick up on the *bandito* business again, and even then, times was tough and outlaw's wages weren't what they used to be.

So Old Pesos Mine got to be just another source of quick income for Paco Serrano; his boys pilfered as much as they politely could, then last visit they came heavier-armed than usual and Paco told me he was borrowing my car, and would return it in a day or so. That was a month back and I hadn't seen the Maxwell again till just now when the half-dozen *banditos* got out of it.

They all slouched behind the car, except for 'Cento who was too big to slouch behind much of anything, and Paco Serrano, who was a different kind from the rest. Paco walked grandly up to the wooden boxes on the bridge and started pushing them to one side. Even dirty and frayed, he had that swaggering way about him, a big man, sad-eyed and mostly stomach, but still big and important-looking. While he came onto the bridge, I stepped behind a crate, unholstered the Harrington, and looked for his brother Tony; he was back of the car, toting his hunting rifle. I glanced over at Ryckman and saw he had sense enough to get behind one crate and in front of another, in the shade between them, to make himself a tricky target. I was in the shade, too, but that was more from habit: found out early on it gets hot in the desert.

"Keep your lookout on the slender one with the rifle," I said to Ryckman.

Then I cocked the Harrington and put a bullet in the bridge at Serrano's feet.

You fire a warning shot like that, there's always a chance somebody will take it wrong and you'll start up a sure-enough gun battle. I didn't like our chances against seven guns, and one of them Tony Serrano, but I figured his boys liked Paco enough not to start shooting with him in the open like he was. But it was a long, tense, second or two, with no sound but the water trickling in the drain ditch, till I knew I'd figured right.

Serrano stopped dead-still at the crack of my pistol, looked mournful, and squinted into the shadow where I was standing. "Is that you, Culley? Is that you and your small gun?"

"It's me, Serrano."

"Is this how you treat an old *amigo, Amigo*?"

"Nice of you to bring my car back—*Amigo*," I said.

A look flickered across his face like he'd forgot where he stole that car from in the first place. Then he brightened up some. "That is true, Culley-Amigo," He almost grinned and raised his voice so his boys could hear, "We are bringing back your fine automobile. We will only move these boxes and drive it over to you." A couple of the boys who'd been hanging behind the car started moving like I guess they might come out eventually.

I thumbed back the hammer and cracked another round, this time into the crate right next to Serrano's hand, and I angled it to splinter the wood. Real showy. Everyone stopped.

"Thanks, but you've done enough," I said, *"Vaya con Dios."*

"Oh, but no, *Amigo,"* he never flinched, just stood there and looked a little sadder, if that was possible, "I have not done enough—," he fingered the splintered crate next to his hand then wiped his fingers on his dirty black coat, "Not nearly enough for this. We will come over, I think."

Well I can't blame him for getting bothered. You go shooting at a man, it's just naturally going to upset him some. Serrano kept his voice polite, but back behind him, 'Cento (His full-given name was Innocent, but no one used it, 'cause he didn't look innocent of anything much.) got a look on his big, gotch-eyed face that said plain enough if he got over that bridge I'd be damn sorry about it.

"I would hate to hurt you, old friend." None of that sentence was true, but I went on, "but you may not come over. And your bravery before my gun has placed you in a poor enough position."

That was true, anyway. And Paco knew it. Standing there in the open, he was sure to be the first or second casualty if any shooting started. And the men behind the car on the other side were looking at the ditch and the barbed-wire fence on my side of it and coming to the sad conclusion that the only way to get here was over the bridge. Yeah, Serrano was in a pretty bad spot just then, but he knew that. He was out there because it was his habit to lead from in front, and his boys liked that about him.

Even now he wasn't going to look scared, and maybe he wasn't. "Perhaps it is not necessary." He went to lean against an empty crate, but it slid away from him, and he had to shuffle a quick two-step to keep his balance. Didn't ruffle him none, though. "We are looking for an old ambulance truck that came possibly by here. Have you maybe seen such a thing?"

"You know damn well I have maybe seen such a thing."

"*Bueno!*" He sighed, "It is well. Back on the Highway, we asked the driver of this truck to stop and talk with us, but—so impolite!—he drove past us and almost killed poor 'Cento! Now we wish only to see what he carries, this truck."

That got to the Dutchman. He'd been quiet till now, but that got to him and he started yelling at Paco. He managed most of it in Spanish, and maybe he didn't know the right words for "thieving bastard" but I guess Serrano caught his drift all right.

"It is sad," Paco shook his head, still leaning against the crate, looking sorry and just a little put out. "Is this right, Culley, that I should endure such insult?"

"My *Gott!*" Ryckman hissed something to me in Dutch, then switched back to Spanish so I understood, "...shot at us... forced off the road... *Banditos!*"

"I know that," I kept my voice low and my Spanish slow and formal, "Do not worry. Just keep watch on that slender gentleman with the long rifle. I can take account of this man. Remember that here is my car he stole."

Then to Serrano I said, "This truck brings machinery to open the mine. You know how long I have waited for it, and he hurried here to bring it to me. He is sorry if in his haste he may have offended you."

"This is undoubtedly true." Serrano knew I was lying, but he relaxed some; it was a good enough story to sop his self-respect and not lose face if he backed off. It wasn't a matter of him trying to look big in front of his men—they didn't believe me any more than he did—but Paco Serrano was a man who commanded a certain amount of respect. That's why he was out in the open while his boys were tucked safe back behind cover. And he had to get that respect. What I just told him was a lie, delivered politely, and if I was right, it was good enough that he wouldn't have to kill us—or try to.

So as he was saying. "This is undoubtedly true," Serrano looked like he just caught his best friend cheating at cards, "But this man should have stopped and showed us this himself. Now, how may I be sure if I do not see the machines?"

That was a good one. Serrano wanted that extra ounce of "aw shucks" and I better give it to him.

"As you well know, *amigo*," I said, "There is but one way for a truck to leave here, which is the way it came. Tomorrow or the next day, this man will set up his machines and he will leave. Then you shall see and hear the machines at work... and you may perhaps meet this gentleman as he leaves, and express your disappointment."

That was it: a guarantee he'd either see the machinery I was lying about or kill Ryckman on the road out. Or maybe both.

"For now," I went on. "This man is my guest. He is frightened by you—and who may blame him? Perhaps it is better you go."

Serrano looked close-to-happy with this. "*Bueno*," he sighed again, "Until that day soon," and he turned to walk back to the car.

We were going to get away with it, whatever it was; I still didn't know what the Dutchman was trucking across the desert.

I didn't relax, though.

And I wish I'd told Ryckman not to.

Because as Serrano walked back to the car, he passed close to his brother Tony and muttered, "Kill the bastard."

CHAPTER 3

Of course, I didn't hear him say "kill the bastard." I just saw him walk closer to Tony than he had to. And watched his lips move. Which was all the warning I needed to hunker down behind my crate and start shooting.

I wasn't near fast enough, though.

In the time it took me to draw a bead, Tony had whipped the hunting rifle to his shoulder and cracked off a round. And Tony Serrano never missed a shot in his life. It was just my good luck he picked the Dutchman.

I heard wood splinter off to that side as Tony's shot went through Ryckman's crate and the Dutchman swore.

And then there was just the shooting.

Times like that it's hard to say just what goes on. I knew Serrano's men were firing at us, but except for Tony, the best of them couldn't hit the ocean if they shot from the beach. And one-eyed 'Cento, the only man I ever saw fire a shotgun with one hand and make it look easy, wasn't much worry at that range. So I just shot at Tony, hoping I could keep him down till I thought of something else.

Then a round whistled past close enough for me to hear it.

Another one kicked up dirt out front of me. Maybe Serrano's boys weren't as blind as I figured, but I tried to ignore that notion and think of something clever.

I was using the Harrington of course. I've fetched a lot of grief over that gun, one way and another, but I wouldn't trade it for nothing. It's a single-action .22 caliber revolver with a seven-inch barrel and a nine-round cylinder. With a barrel that long, you can hit anything you aim at up to sixty yards, and for close-in work, the muzzle velocity of a round coming out of that much barrel will stop a big man dead in his tracks and knock a small one clean over—especially if you put a little notch in the soft tip of the bullet. Don't ask me how I know that trick. And with nine rounds in the cylinder, you don't hardly have to re-load at all. I've known some tough guys who wouldn't shoot anything smaller than a .45, but I shot plenty of that high-caliber stuff in the Army, and I never liked it much, so, I stick with the Harrington, and it's never let me down.

So there I was, firing at Tony, who had sense enough to stay down where I couldn't get him. Off to my left, I heard the Dutchman's rifle and figured he wasn't too bad hit. I'd fired two warning shots at Serrano early on, remember, and I spent four more on Tony, which left me with three. I had a pocketful of cartridges in my shirt pocket, but I didn't figure anyone was going to stop and let me re-load, so I ought to think of something pretty soon, but nothing come to mind.

And right then, someone landed a shot in the crate right next to my face and put a good-size splinter in my cheek.

Damn, it hurt.

It knocked me back for a second, and that was all the time Tony needed to stand and line up on me. I saw him doing it. In slow motion. He was behind my car, maybe 30-40 yards off, the muzzle of his hunting rifle looking big and close enough to stick me in the eye with it. I tried to fall back and raise and fire the Harrington at the same time, but I never was any good at that sort of thing, and like I say, Tony Serrano never missed a shot in his life.

Next thing I was falling over on my ass and wondering if this was when I should start that my-whole-life-passing-before-my-eyes thing, but what I saw then was something completely else: It was the flash from Tony's muzzle, of course, but just a split-second before that, something exploded at his left shoulder, his rifle jerked up, and I felt the bullet ruffle past as Tony's round parted my hair.

I just kept falling, naturally, and didn't hear the actual shot till my butt smacked gravel.

It had come from behind me.

And four more right after it.

I rolled over and took a look backward.

It was Ray, the Dutchman's driver. He'd dropped into the drain channel that runs down from the cliff face and snuck down alongside the truck path, and he was sitting there in that shallow culvert pumping lead from his Winchester in a way that looked pretty discouraging to Paco and his friends.

I could see right away that from where he was perched, he'd be awful hard for even a good shot to hit—and I said before, most of those guys couldn't hit darkness at sunset. But from his spot, Ray could kill or cripple a few of them, disable my car, and cut off their retreat.

I just hoped he had sense enough not to.

CHAPTER 4

An hour later we laid Ryckman on the cot in my office shack. He was breathing shallow and trying not to cough, but his eyes were clear and he could talk good enough.

The Serranos had cleared out—in my car—so we had some time. Ray looked around the office, taking in the made-up cot, the fresh-swept floor, and the neat stacks of everything that could be neatly stacked. Didn't take him a second. Then, without a word, he fired up the shiny wood stove to boil water while I cut away the Dutchman's shirt. Ray peered over my shoulder to see the wound.

It was low on the left side of his chest, a clean puncture. Good so far. But then Ryckman coughed, a little bubble of pink blood oozed out of his mouth and popped silently to trickle down his chin. Ryckman felt it and said something in Dutch that sounded like:

"Goddammittohellanyway."

We all looked at each other, and the ugly scar upside Ray's mouth got deeper and uglier. But we couldn't think of anything to add to what the Dutchman said.

Coughing blood meant Ryckman got himself hit in the lung, and that meant right here and right now, he was good as dead.

I've got to say he took it well—better than some I've seen: I mean, a man's dying, you hate to criticize how he goes about it, but I've seen some folks do it all wrong. All of it wrong. But Ryckman just looked around the room, his eyes focused on my bookshelf, and he said:

"Have you a Bible?" in his bad Spanish.

"I have," I answered, "But it is in English."

He gave a look like *That figures*, but he said, "Might I hold it?" and I went to dig it out.

Myself, I can't see why a dying man would want to read the Bible anyway. Seems to me you'll get plenty of that Bible stuff in Heaven. Lots of Christians up there, they tell me, and most of them pretty religious. And if I understand this eternity thing right, you'll get plenty of their company. No sense practicing up for it here on Earth. Nossir, when I die, I want to be reading BLACK MASK magazine, or something else fairly entertaining, but maybe I'll see it different when my time comes. I rooted around for the Bible, and Ray took the kettle off the stove and shut it down while Ryckman talked to him in Dutch or something.

When I handed the Bible to Ryckman, it sounded like they'd decided something. He took it from me and leafed through it.

"Since two years I have not read this," he fought back a cough, then said, "You are go to see in the back of the truck."

"He means he wants you to see what we're carrying in the ambulance," Ray explained in his perfect English, "I parked it where you said I should."

I didn't go right away; thought I should give them some time for second thoughts, and besides my face hurt. I picked out the splinter some lucky-shot *bandito* had put in my cheek and dabbed some mercurochrome on it. Then I looked at them like, "You're sure?" and they nodded. I headed out towards the cliff.

As I left the office shack, I automatically glanced at the spur road. The last dust from Serrano's car—which used to be my car—had long faded out over the horizon. I didn't like that much; meant he was hurrying when he didn't have to.

Anyway, I walked up the packed yellow-clay road to the cliff face and into the tunnel under the overhang where Ray had left the ambulance. There was a coal-oil lantern just inside the opening and I fixed it up to see my way inside and into the back of the ambulance.

Only I didn't look in the back right away; I checked in the cab first, just being contrary, I guess. There was a pair of Army .45 automatics in there, and two sawed-off double-barrel shotguns. Extra clips for the .45s and shells taped around the butts of the shotguns. Also, there was extra ammunition for the Dutchman's carbine and Ray's Winchester.

Looked to me like these gentlemen maybe were ready for a little trouble.

With that in mind, I went around back and opened the doors to look inside.

It was full of Gold.

Well, maybe a quarter or one-third full. There was a lot of Gold anyway. All in little ten-pound bars, neatly taped and stacked in straight rows on each side, where the ambulance floor was strongest, and braced there with two-by-fours. I peeled back the tape and picked one up, and the feel of it—the heavy, slick *feel* of it—was like an electric charge running up my arm.

A sight like that can change a man. I was standing in front of more money than had come out of this mine in four hundred years, all just sitting right in front of me. Damn funny-feeling. Part of it was thinking of what all that money can buy: quiet cars and soft beds and cool, sweet drinks at shiny bars where the boy calls you "sir" and women across the room notice your expensive clothes and smile for you. But another part was just Gold—shiny-bright yellow Gold!

Then the lantern flickered out. And it came to me that I was standing in a crummy, worked-out mine shaft somewhere between Nowhere and Nothing, with someone else's truckload of trouble and a half-dozen Mexican bandits up the road there ready to kill me for it.

Kind of snapped me back, it did.

There was plenty of light to find my way out, and I put back the Gold bar and walked out in the sun.

When I got back to the office, Ray was cleaning the rifles—or rather, he'd broke them down and soaked them in gunpowder solvent, and while he waited for the metal to sweat it out, he was checking on the Dutchman and looking over my bookshelves. The scar that twisted his mouth was almost invisible when his face relaxed, but as soon as I came in, it deepened again, like he got tense with people around.

Ryckman was still leafing through the Bible, looking for a familiar name maybe, and I could see he was having a little more trouble breathing. He looked up as I entered and tried a smile and some more bad Spanish:

"You keep a house clean," he said.

"I have been long alone," I could speak better Spanish than that, but I kept it slow and stilted for his sake. "A man alone must keep everything in cleanliness or allow all to go to ruin. I prefer cleanliness." He nodded and I went on, "Now I must ask: The bandits—do they know of the Gold?"

He shook his head "no" and cleared his throat with a deep, ugly rumble. Concentrated on holding that Bible till he could breathe again, and finally, he looked back up at me.

"This is of important," he managed in Spanish, "That you should know I have of this Gold, come by it honestly." He held the Bible kind of tighter and swallowed, hard. "There are those who will say I abandoned my Savior, and some will say I did it for Gold. But-" swallowed again. "-Did Christ want me to leave her there? In that awful place?"

"Hard to say," I said.

"You are a religious man?"

"I try to be," I lied. Then I remembered something I once heard Seamus Feeney say to a dying bootlegger: "Many men say they know the mind of God. And what they know, they no longer seek to learn. The important thing is to never stop seeking to learn what is His will for us to do. It is not always understood."

Not by me, anyway; I ain't been in a church since Christ was a Corporal, but there was no point bringing that up right now.

What I did say seemed to please Ryckman though. Maybe he wasn't expecting much. He got some kind of God-awful look on his face like he was trying to smile or something, and he said in Spanish, "I was—"

Then he stopped real quick and his eyes went wide all of a sudden: panicky-like. For a few seconds he fought between not-breathing and not-coughing, like a man underwater aches to fill his lungs and knows it'll kill him if he does. There was a nasty sound in his chest. Then another.

Ray moved over by the cot, and Ryckman grabbed his arm and started talking, low and fast, in Dutch. Ray looked up from him, over to me. And the Dutchman kept talking.

CHAPTER 5

I can't write it like he told it.

For one thing, I don't speak Dutch, and that's what he talked, mostly. I didn't understand any of it without Ray to translate the words for me. But the tone in Ryckman's voice left no mistaking: he knew he was dying and he wanted to get this said.

And I don't know how to put it across, that look in his eyes that wasn't quite pleading, but hurting just to be understood. I can't tell it just right about the sound in his voice: like this was important, and he wanted pretty bad for me to hear it. There was Ray, kneeling beside the cot, the Dutchman talking fast and panicky, and Ray putting it slow and careful into English...

...and it seems this Mijnheer Ryckman, he's a jeweler, from a family of jewelers. A good family in Amsterdam, he says. Old and honorable, their business prosperous and well-respected, and he

works hard and he's looked on with a fair amount of favor where he comes from.

I guess his business takes him to Berlin back in '32, which is when the Nazis are getting to be a big noise over there, and they're starting in to give the Jews a hard way to go, and Ryckman, he can see there's money to be made out of a situation like this, so slowly, over the next few years, he gets a sideline going, buying jewelry from the Jewish—the old Jewish mostly.

And Gold.

He says the Jewish would rather deal with their people, but he's friendly to them, which is important, and he deals honest, which is more important, and so when a lot of the Germans get finicky all of a sudden about what-all Jews can buy and sell, Mijnheer Ryckman gets a reputation as a safe gentile to do business with.

Funny thing, though: after a while, Ryckman gets to know these Jews, and then he gets to know them better and one day he wakes up and finds out he kind of likes them, which isn't real well thought-of back in Amsterdam, and it's a getting a damnsight unfashionable there in Berlin. But Janse Ryckman, he just can't help it on account of—

He stopped talking here and made a funny sound, kind of like swallowing before he could go on.

- on account of he meets up with a Jewish banker named Shlomo Rosenstern, and this old man has a daughter Rebecca, and Ryckman decides he wants her for his wife.

The way Ryckman talked about this woman he married; it was like the sun come up every morning just to get a look at her. And later on, when we went through his things, I saw he carried her picture in his wallet, and I had to admit she was pretty nice to see: dark hair in loose waves, big soft eyes, and kind of a funny mouth—maybe the way she smiled, I don't know. Looked like a woman you'd go to some trouble for.

And the way Rykman tells it, there's plenty of that -- trouble, I mean. Ryckman's hard-working and honest, and I guess the Rosentern girl can see this, and he's good-looking too, which don't hurt none. And before long her father, old Shlomo Rosenstern, he's doing a fit because his daughter wants to marry a fair-haired gentile.

The Dutchman went all of a sudden into a shot of coughing and like to never stop. Ray wiped his forehead with the arm that Ryckman wasn't holding onto, and I saw then that all this talk was hard on him—on Ray, I mean, it was hard on him some way.

I wondered about that, but it didn't look like he'd have to do it much longer. Then the Dutchman somehow got hold, held his breath a minute, and went on.

He says again how he's a gentile, and fair-haired, and right about then in Berlin, there's these gangs of big, brown-shirt Nazis, big men with blonde hair—all blonde, like Mijnheer Ryckman—look just like him, and going around in gangs beating up on Jews in the street. Robbing, tormenting, and kicking the crutches out from under old ladies when they think it's safe I guess. So Shlomo forbids his daughter Rebecca from marrying Ryckman.

And just like you'd figure, that means they can't stay apart.

Ryckman converts to their religion. Becomes Jewish so they can marry in the eyes of her people. He turns his back on his old Church and his family, and he does this for Rebecca, so her old man will let them get married, and old Rosenstern accepts it because he has to.

Never likes it much, though.

And in Ryckman's family, it's worse.

I guess the folks back home in Amsterdam, they been talking already about him dealing so much with the Jews, and now they say he's betrayed Jesus: sold out on his Savior for some Jew's Gold. He lets them say it. He loves this woman, and she loves him right back, so he breaks from his family and he breaks from his friends and becomes man-and-wife with Rebecca in a Jewish ceremony, with old Shlomo looking on, rolling his eyes at the whole mess.

Damn it was strange, kind of, hearing this guy Ray tell all about this other man's life, all this personal stuff, and Ray just saying the words like he was reading names from a phone book. I took a look out the window, towards the spur road. Nothing showing. Maybe the Serrano boys just decided to call the whole thing off. Or maybe not...

Way out there, just shy of where the road vanished on the horizon, and the sky shimmered in the heat, there was something out there. Hard to tell just what it was, from this far away and in all that sun, but it looked like someone moving around in the rocks, trying to find a shady spot to watch from.

And the Dutchman still talked while Ray translated:

Ryckman says the next thing he does is get his wife out of Germany. This is maybe around '34 and it isn't hard then, not like it is now, and Rebecca wants her father to come with them, but the old man won't go. Not then. Ryckman's got no business left in Holland now, no friends nor any family to speak to him. They take a boat to Vera Cruz, and try to get into the States. He has money to start a small jewelry business and they go north to Tijuana, to be closer to the USA, and he says they make a good living, even in the hard times, and what he says is that a woman like Rebecca makes even bad times all right, and the good times... I don't know what he said about that; Ray just kind of trailed off for a few beats, listening to Ryckman talk about his woman. Hearing how he talked about her.

But they finally do get into the States and about that time (This would be early in '35 I guess) Adolph Hitler's been running things back in the Fatherland for a few years now. Ryckman recalls how right after Hitler took over, a man named Albert Einstein left Germany real sudden. But I guess you don't have to be Einstein to see which way the grass is growing over there, especially not when one of the first things Hitler did was to build a place called Dachau.

Yeah, and one day Shlomo gets beat up and his store smashed in by the Nazis, and he decides it's time he should come live with his relatives in America. And he talks his friends into it, and relations, and I guess it ends up quite a few of them decide to get the hell out while they can. So they convert their wealth and valuables and property into Gold, and then they get it out of Germany and over here.

And now they need to sell it.

That's when all of a sudden old Rosenstern figures that having a big, strong, goyish son-in-law in America ain't such a bad thing; they got to get a fair price for that Gold over here, and Ryckman knows the business and has the connections...

Right then there was more coughing from Ryckman. Only it was more like a deep-down gurgle. I could hear his lung filling up pretty bad and I wondered for a time how he'd ever go on talking, but I guess this was important for him to say it. Ray picked out the words as best as he could, but it got confused: *Shlomo and his people made passage... all their*

Gold here... something about the Police... They had all this Gold but they had to sell it quick and there was only one way to do it right: something about a rich Grandee named Escachza de Samaniego, just outside Guanajuato, down south of here, he'd promised to buy the Gold on good terms.

All Ryckman had to do was get it there. Down to Guanajuato.

Ryckman stopped talking. Not coughing now, but trying not to cough.

I looked over at Ray.

"We were on the main road from Saltillo to Guanajuato last night," Ray said, "When we ran into that bunch you call the Serrano brothers. *Mijnheer* Ryckman says you know of them."

"You could say that," I nodded. "I guess they took up running a Midnight Tollbooth along that stretch of highway north of here."

"Here" being old Pesos Mine. The way he told it, Ray tried to drive around Serrano's men and ended up on the spur road going down here to Old Pesos. I don't know what they did to slow up the Serrano brothers, but judging by the lead they had, it must have been something pretty saucy. They would have got clean away if the spur road went anyplace else, but all it did was smack up against the cliff face here at Old Pesos.

And here they were.

Ryckman tried to talk some more, but he wasn't much good at it now, and when Ray could understand him at all it was just him repeating parts—parts where he talked about his wife, how he left his Church and his family for her, lost his friends. And folks back home said he got corrupted by Jewish Gold and turned his back on his Savior. He'd been the fair-haired boy back there, but he gave it all up, and he wasn't a bit sorry for any of it. He'd do it again if he had the chance because Rebecca was worth every bit of it. Only...

"...Only if he could have done this with the Gold," Ray translated. "Sold the Gold I guess he means—to make her father and his people not so ashamed of his daughter. With *Mijnheer* Ryckman's family, it's finished, and what they think of him, he doesn't care, but a woman like Rebecca, he says she should have her people to be proud of her and not make her feel disgraced for marrying him.

"This Gold, selling it to the man in Guanajuato and bringing back the money, that was his chance to bring pride to his wife, and do a good turn for her people, and... he says all he did is to ruin it. He says he's going to leave his bones here in the desert, and—it's some kind of Dutch expression, like 'that's just too damn bad' or something—but losing the Gold and shaming his wife, it's hard for him to think on."

And it was tough to see him, coughing to death and wrought up about his woman like that.

So Ray and I told him to rest easy; we'd see it got done for him.

Ray said it in Dutch and I used slow, clear Spanish, so he'd understand and no mistakes.

The way he looked at us then, it's hard to tell it. I mean, to me that promise was just some words I said to ease his troubling mind, but Ryckman took it for real. Dying men don't look happy, and he was sure enough dying, so he didn't smile. He just looked like we took a load off his mind and now he could get where he was going a little easier.

Something like that, I guess.

He didn't say "Thanks," he just asked in Spanish, "You are sure?" and we told him we were sure. He swallowed another cough, took a few quick, shallow breaths, then started in with instructions: Samaniego's ranch outside Guanajuato and how to get there; the contracts in the ambulance and the agreed price "Samaniego," he kept saying it, "Samaniego, Samaniego..." he broke up coughing, then, "In dollars," he said the best he could, "Not Pesos. And no Bank Drafts. Banks are—"

And that was pretty much the last thing he said. He started coughing up blood, and there was no help for it. We stuck close by and held onto his arms so he knew he wasn't alone. But he didn't last long till he went all limp and we heard what they call the "death rattle," which is the sound air makes bubbling up through lungs full of blood.

And that was it.

"Guess he finished his story," I said.

"No," Ray looked down at him, and as I tried to figure out the look on his twisted face, he said, "He passed it on. To us."

CHAPTER 6

R ay went back to the table and wiped off the gun parts he'd been cleaning. Reassembled the rifles while I opened a can of peaches—that's how fast he did it—and we ate some.

Sounds cold-blooded, I know, to eat in front of a dead man, but it was getting on close to noon and I don't think either one of us had eaten since last night. I sure hadn't anyway. And I wanted to mention to Ray about where I got those peaches, but before I could think to do it, we were done eating; we wiped our mouths and went back to Ryckman. He'd pretty much bled clear through that cot of mine so we wrapped him in the sheet on the bed, tucking it tight around him.

"I guess we should bury him." I couldn't think of anything else to say, not knowing if Ray had been a good friend of his or anything. "There's plenty of half-dug pits out around here, and we can cover him decent."

Ray didn't say anything, just stood there looking at the sheet-wrapped body.

"And I think I read someplace about Jews have to be buried by sundown according to their religion," I added.

That seemed to snap Ray out of it a little. But he still just stood there looking, and we didn't have a lot of time for that. Finally, he said: "You think *Mijnheer* Ryckman became a Christian again? There before he died?" He moved around to the foot of the cot and I moved to the head.

"I hope not." We both lifted. "The way I see it, turning Jewish was the most Christian thing he ever done."

Ryckman wasn't too heavy for us and Ray carried his end all right as we steered him out the door.

"And he sure enough loved that woman," I went on, "to give the razzberry to his folks and everybody, marry her and get her out of Germany like that. Which was another good thing he done, from what I hear. Getting her out of Germany, I mean."

"I guess you're right," Ray followed me, holding the foot of the cot with its dead burden. It was sort of awkward, trying to see behind me and walk over the rough-gravel ground, but we managed all right, and I steered us toward someplace in the shade by the cliff face where there were some pits already half-dug.

"Bad place for Jews just now," I said, trying to talk, walk backward and carry a dead man all to once. "Germany, I mean: bad place for Jews. And it's going to get worse, what I figure. Nossir, I'd hate to think he fell in love with this woman so hard like that, did so much good for her and her folks—then turned his back on it all at the end and repented it like something he was ashamed of."

"Good point I guess," Ray nodded and hitched up his end of the cot. "But the way he clutched that Bible... and he was raised a Christian. Sometimes, when a man is dying, he fears the next life bad enough to turn his back, like you say, on what he should be most proud of."

"You a religious man yourself?" I didn't want to step on his feelings any if he was. But he didn't answer right away. Didn't say anything. We'd reached a good hole, big enough and deep enough to hold Ryckman's body—he wasn't the kind of man to put in a shallow grave—but not too big and deep to fill. We set the cot down next to the hole, both of us moving at the same time, like we'd practiced it.

One thing I've learned through the years: Dead men are heavy. I guess Ray knew it too because we both got down in that hole ourselves—it was maybe chest-deep to me, shoulder-deep for Ray—before we picked up the cot again and then lowered Ryckman in as gentle as we could. Finally, when we climbed out of the hole, Ray said,

"I don't know. I was religious once, I guess. Maybe I will be again."

"That's not a bad thing," I grunted, put a hand on my lower back, and straightened up. "I just never could see this business about believing in God so you won't go to Hell."

"Many people do. Who can blame them?"

"Nope. Never could see it."

We fetched shovels from a place near the cliff face where I had them stowed and walked back to the hole in the ground that was now a grave. "You figure Heaven's like that? Full of folks who got there just 'cause they was scared of burning in Hell?" I guess I didn't ask it like I wanted an answer, because Ray didn't say nothing, and I went on, "Way I figure, religion's like a magazine," I said, "You buy it because you like the editorial policy, or it's got good stories in it, or maybe it's just the picture on the cover; not because you're scared of the publisher."

"Maybe you're right."

Neither one of us could think of anything else to say over Ryckman's body. So, we just started shoveling loose gravel into the Dutchman's grave.

"Some things I'm still not clear about in my mind," I said after we'd been working a time.

"I thought there might be."

On the other side of the grave, Ray was likewise shoveling, and we were starting to raise a fair amount of dust.

"If you don't mind what may be an awkward question," I moved some more dirt. "Can you tell me just exactly how you come to be driving up to my door just now with a truck full of Gold? Our friend here wasn't real detailed on that, or maybe I just didn't understand him too good."

"*Mijnheer* Ryckman's father-in-law, this man Rosenstern." Ray kept shoveling while he talked. Ryckman was covered now, and that would have been good enough for some folks I know, but we wanted to fill the hole clear to the top. "He and a lot of his people decided to leave Germany and they had to get their money out, mostly in Gold. And I guess if you're going to move a whole lot of Gold from Germany to America, you can't just stick a stamp on it and put it in the mailbox. There seem to be a lot of laws about it—especially for Jews in Germany these days."

We kept working, and between us, the hole was starting to fill up while Ray explained:

"But Rosenstern's people have got some way of getting around things like that; a tradition, almost. And there was an awful lot of them in on this thing. Anyway, this Rosenstern—Ryckman's father-in-law—he got a Swiss friend of his to take possession of all this *gelt* in Germany and transfer ownership of a like amount to a Jew in Switzerland who has connections with a Jew in England, whose cousins run an exchange in Canada, and in few weeks, old Rosenstern and a few dozen of his kith and kin owned a half a ton of Gold up in California."

"I've heard of things like that," I wiped dusty sweat from my brow, took a quick glance at the spur road—was there movement out there, a mile or so out? — and went back to shoveling. "From what I saw in the ambulance, I guess it worked pretty good."

"But there were still problems." Ray spat a mouthful of dust, "More problems. Seems just about the time Rosenstern and his people got possession of all that Gold up in the States, they found out President Roosevelt had gone and passed a law against owning it."

I hadn't heard about that, but then I'd been out of touch a while.

"A law against owning Gold? FDR done that?"

"A few years ago, I guess. Said it was the only way to get a handle on the economy or something like that."

"Maybe so, but I guess that kicked old Rosenstern's retirement plans under the outhouse floor."

"U.S. Treasury probably would have seized it if the Gold had got here legally," Ray said, "But it didn't get here legally and that meant Rosenstern and his friends had to get rid of it in a hurry. And they didn't have any way to sell it in the States except on the Black Market, where they might be lucky to get maybe half what it was worth."

"Prices was better down here?"

We just about had the grave filled by now. I added a couple more shovels-full while Ray smoothed it out.

"*Mijnheer* Ryckman was a jeweler, remember," Ray said, "And he knew there was a pretty brisk trade from Americans pushing their Gold south to sell it in the border towns like Tia Juana and Mexicali before the Government shut them down. But Ryckman figured he could get a better price further south, in Guanajuato. So he set up this deal with this fellow, Don Escachza de Samaniego—I guess he's a big *ranchero* in those parts, and he agreed to buy all the Gold." Ray patted the earth down one last time. "All he had to do was get it there."

The grave was filled by now so I guessed the funeral was pretty much done. Ray turned to me. I thought he might want to say something else, and maybe he tried. But he just went on,

"Ryckman, like he said, this was his big chance to get his wife back in good graces with her family. He took on the job of transporting the Gold to Guanajuato and he hired me and my truck for it," he finished.

"Makes sense, I guess," I said. Nothing much for me to add, except, "What now?"

"Now we think of a way to get the Gold to this Samaniego in Guanajuato."

I was getting used to that ugly face of his by now—how the scar gave him that twisted smile, and made him look sarcastic when he spoke.

But what he said was just fact.

CHAPTER 7

We walked back to the office shack. "I been thinking on that myself," I said, "And what-all we're supposed to do about that Gold here now. Like you said, I don't figure we can just put a stamp on it and drop it in the mail. You got any other ideas?"

While we were burying Ryckman, we'd both had a chance to look out to the horizon some, and seen the dust on the spur road coming back this way now. Which would be the Serrano brothers and whoever else they could carry, coming on slow, so they could lay up in the close-by rocks till they felt like calling.

"I suppose driving out the way we came is out of the question," Ray said.

"Pretty near." I opened the office door and we went in, out of the sun. "Looks to me like the Serrano brothers got men camped out on some of the high ground over there, and if I know their style, they probably rolled heavy rocks across the road where they'll do them some good."

Ray nodded, looked out the window, down the gravel slope, and across to the spur road. He'd come that way, remember, he'd seen the country, and he knew as well as me there was no way to get that heavy-loaded ambulance back to the highway except by the spur. Neither one of us liked it much, but there it was: We couldn't drive out.

And it looked like we could expect company sometime tonight or whenever the boys felt sociable.

"What are our chances of holding them off here?" he asked.

"Damn slim, I'd say. You're sure they don't know what you're carrying?"

"I don't see how," Ray looked thoughtful, "Possible, I guess, but I don't think so," he grinned, kind of, and it made his mouth twist up ugly-like. "If they knew about all that Gold, they'd never have backed off like they did. But they damnsure know there's something here."

"You got a point there. And by the way, thanks for not forcing their hand back at the bridge there. I wasn't in a real good shooting spot for a long fight. You were, but I wasn't."

"Neither was *Mijnheer* Ryckman, I'm afraid," he studied out the window a little more. "And you don't think this is a better position?"

"Better," I said, "But still a long way from good enough," I pointed to a squat little building that used to house a steam engine, just across the clay road going up to the cliff wall. "The Engine Shack over there is the strongest defense point, and we got food and water enough to stay awhile, but so do the Serrano Brothers. And they can get more if they decide to wait us out. But I don't think they will," I pointed down the slope to the bridge. "Come dark, they can slip across that bridge, them and their boys, and we can't stop them," I traced a line with my finger up the gravel slope past the few sheds and storage buildings around us. "Plenty of cover if they need it, but they'll probably just move close up in the dark, throw gasoline all over everything and torch us out."

"How many do you think?" Ray looked out the other window, up at the cliff and the tunnels where ore had been dug out. "Could we pick them off from up there?"

"They'll probably bring back some fresh hands with them. With the three brothers... let's say less than a dozen, but not much less. We could pick off a few, but then when they had our position, they could move up in the dark. And the last time I counted, there was just the two of us."

"That's about what I count too," he nodded, "Is there any dynamite around?"

"This ain't that kind of operation," You can't kill anyone with dynamite anyway, except by mistake, but there was no point going into that, since we didn't have any.

"Just a one-man outfit?" Ray gave me a cautious look like he maybe wondered what the hell I was doing out here anyway, but didn't want to pry.

"It wasn't supposed to be," I said, "Back in '29 when times were good, a company called Kurtz, Ltd. sent me down to Mexico to look at the gravel here at the Old Pesos Mine. You can separate good silver from low-grade by pouring nitric acid on it, but the notion was slow catching on down hereabouts; some folks think it's bad for the soil, the water, or something."

"You mean it's not?"

"Well, it probably don't do it much good," I looked out the window at the miles and miles of ugly ground as far as the eye could see. "But hell, ain't nobody going to start living around here, so I guess it don't hurt nothing."

Years later, when little babies started growing up dead, folks thought a lot different about pouring poison over the water table, but back when I'm writing about we didn't know any better. And bad as we needed money back then, I'm not sure we would have done it any different even if we did know. "Old man Kurtz bought an option on this place and sent a bright young mining engineer name of Vernon Culley—that's me—down here to test the gravel and see if it was worth dumping acid on."

"You're a mining engineer?"

"Yeah, I got me a degree and everything. From a good college, too. I wrote back to Kurtz he could make a decent profit here if he didn't spend too much money on it, and he wrote back to ask, 'How cheap could it get done?' and I wrote back he could fix up most of the machines, get gas to run them, and maybe hire some fellows to shovel it up and ship it out, and he wrote back to ask, 'Could I do it as long as I was down here anyway?' and I wrote back I could do anything, as long as he wasn't fussy about it, so he sent me down some money, and I bought gas and supplies and started fixing things up."

"Looks like work all right," Ray looked around my office. It was neat and organized okay, but I guess there wasn't much to it. "How far did you get with it?"

"Just got started," I said, "And then the bottom dropped out of everything: Stock Market crashed, money dried up, and it all went to Hell. I had to lay off the men I hired, my pay got kind of spotty, Kurtz lost the Mine, and here I been ever since, just trying to make up my mind to up and move out."

Ray chewed on this. "Have you made up your mind?"

We could both see out the window that cloud of dust earlier was bigger now and just like we figured, it was the Serrano boys coming back in my Maxwell. They looked to be laying up in the rocks just a couple hundred yards on the other side of the bridge. Till dark, anyway.

"Guess things is kind of come to a head on that issue."

"You don't think we can stand them off here, do you?" Ray kept looking out the window, thoughtful-like.

"I wouldn't care for the odds, no."

"You have another idea?"

"I got just one," Something was coming to me, or maybe I was just making it up as I went along. "Nothing brilliant, and I don't like it much, and if you got a better one, I'm glad to listen, but it's an idea."

Ray looked at the shadows and figured how much daylight we had left. A few hours maybe.

"Will it take long, this idea of yours?"

"There's a dozen shafts back in that cliff where we could hide the Gold—and maybe three or four where we could get it back out pretty easy."

"So we hide the Gold?"

"And then we get ourselves out of here."

"You mean leave it all behind?"

"That's my notion. If you're right, the Serrano boys won't know to look for it. You and me get to the closest town, then we come back with plenty of help. Guns and the men to use them. But, like I said, if you've got a better idea, I'm a reasonable man."

Ray chewed his lip a minute and that scar upside his mouth twisted his face around. Then he turned away from the window and scanned my bookshelf again. Like he could see something important there. Finally, he nodded and said, "We get out of here, and where do we go for help?"

One thing a mine has plenty of is maps. I pulled one out of a neat stack and unfolded it across the table.

"We could slip past the Serrano boys in the dark and maybe get back to the highway—east of here—but that's kind of dicey," I explained. Ray nodded, remembering the terrain between the mine and the highway. "Besides," I said, "Paco will figure us to go that way, and we'd be easy to follow. But there's a footpath to get to the top of the cliff behind us. And from there, we head west, it's maybe forty miles across the desert to... lessee..." I squinted at a little dot on the map, near a fairly-traveled road, "Closest place... Quenada. You know it?"

I'd swear he winced, but it was hard reading that face of his.

"I know the place," he nodded, "The locals call it 'Nada.' Which seems to fit."

"They have any law there?"

"They have law," again the nasty look. "A man named Milianos."

"He any good?" I could see there was something about Quenada Ray didn't care to discuss. "Should we make for someplace else?"

"He's good enough." Ray looked down at the map like a man holding a worthless hand of cards. Even on a table-size map, that stretch of desert looked awful big and empty. "And there's no place other," he sighed at last, "We must go to 'Nada."

"You sure?"

If there was some good reason not to go there, I figured he'd tell me about it. But he just nodded again.

"There's no place other," he repeated. He looked from the map back up to me. "You can walk forty miles across the desert?"

"I've walked maybe half that. Twenty miles. Took me a day, mostly."

Funny things a man'll do when he's alone and has read all the books around: one day I took my map and compass and walked ten miles out into the desert and ten miles back. Did it a couple of times more, with a squirrel rifle so I could call it hunting, but basically it was just walking away the time.

"It would be perhaps two days to 'Nada?" Ray asked.

"More likely three if we travel by night. Night's cooler, and there's going to be enough moon to see by. And I heard there's water comes out at night that you don't get in the daytime. Yeah, three days, if we detour to a water hole I know-" I poked a spot on the map. "You feel like a walk?"

CHAPTER 8

Dropping the Gold down a mineshaft wasn't near as hard as that sounds. There was plenty of gear in the tunnels for moving ore by the ton—pulleys, winches, and carts —and the Dutchman had crated and packed his gold to be carried easy. Once we got it down a shaft in a cart we could pull up again someday, we dropped rocks and dust—which is another thing a mine has plenty of—down over it till the shaft looked pretty well forgotten. Then Ray squeezed his empty ambulance up a connecting tunnel to a good spot maybe three mine shafts away, close to some likely-looking hiding places the Serrano boys could spend their time searching through.

For good measure, I hauled up some heavy machinery still in its crate and loaded it into the back of the ambulance. That would back up my story to Paco about what Ryckman had been trucking here. Probably wouldn't fool him much, but he'd appreciate the effort. Ray meantime took the spark plugs out of the engine and hid them good. "We're okay to pack up now." I put a note on the windshield:

SERRANO,

I'll BE BACK IN A WEEK. WAIT FOR ME.

CULLEY

Then I turned back to Ray, "You want anything from inside the cab here?"

"Just the guns and ammunition."

"They'll be a load to carry, across a desert."

"Maybe," Ray looked thoughtful, twisting his crooked mouth up till it was near sideways on his face. "But I hate to leave it all here for those two-bit bad guys to shoot at us. Maybe we can hide it all someplace on our way?"

This was a better idea than I knew at the time, but right then it was just something not worth arguing about. I shrugged and helped carry guns back to the office shack. Like I said before, there were two double-barrel shotguns, sawed-off short; a pair of U.S. Army .45 automatics, and maybe twenty pounds of ammunition. Too much to carry across a desert but—Ray was right—too much to leave for the Serranos to shoot back at us.

Back in the office shack, we packed Ray's Winchester and the Dutchman's carbine in a duffle bag, along with the scatterguns and ammunition. Ray holstered one of the .45s, strapped it on his belt, and offered me the other one.

"No thanks," I patted the Harrington in its holster on my hip and stuck a couple boxes of .22s in my pockets. "I'm comfortable with this."

Ray nodded. "A man should shoot what he's comfortable with."

Right then he went up another grade in my book. I been catching grief over that Harrington for years, mostly from tough guys who think a .22's not enough gun; they say you can't put a man down with a .22 round, and they say it loud, and I used to put up with a lot of that because it wasn't worth the powder to show just how wrong they could be about a thing like that. But a man who carries a .45 and still respects a .22 shows pretty good judgment in my opinion. I guess that's when I started to appreciate Ray.

It's funny. You'd think him pulling my ass out of that scrape down there at the bridge would have made me like him some, but just showing up with a rifle don't make you a friend. I fought alongside men back in the war that wouldn't cross the street to spit on me, so I know a little about fighting and maybe something about friendship. That came later.

Meanwhile, we stuffed canned meat and crackers in a bag, filled canteens from the well in the engine shack, then—the way you will before you leave a place—looked around to see if we forgot something.

Ray turned to me. "The Serrano brothers-" he started, hesitated, then: "-and their men: Are they the kind who will wreck this place when they see we are gone? Just to wreck it?"

"Pretty likely," I nodded. "Why? Anything here you want?"

He walked over to the shelves and pulled off a few books. NOSTROMO and VICTORY. GREAT EXPECTATIONS. PERSUASION. THE COUNT OF MONTE CRISTO. Others. Books that had been friends to me all that time alone in the desert.

He held up a book of poems by Emily Dickinson. "Is this any good?"

"Try one."

He opened it. Read:

"God gave a loaf to every bird,
But just a crumb to me,"

Closed it and put it back on the shelf. Then, like a kid snitching candy, he gently laid in two issues of BLACK MASK.

It's hard to explain how it made me feel. When you're alone in the desert with just the occasional Mexican bandit for conversation and company, books get to be pretty important to you. Sometimes they're the only friends you got, and you even visit the dull ones more than once. These books had been about my only real company for a few years now, but I had been going to leave them rather than look foolish. Ray saved them. Which is how we got to be friends.

"Good choices." We put the books in the bag with the arms and ammunition, "Let me help you carry that." And as we climbed up the footpath to the top of the cliff – and the desert beyond – I told Ray how I got the peaches.

CHAPTER 9

Yeah, the canned peaches. The ones Ray and I ate before we buried the Dutchman. I better tell about them. I'm not a fast-thinking man, but I get there in my own good time, and it finally struck me how they might have something to do with all this.

It was a couple days before Ray and the Dutchman showed up, this German guy comes along. I'm in the office shack trying to fill up some time sweeping and stacking things I'd swept and stacked a dozen times before when I hear this noise... thought it was a loud car at first, but not exactly. The sound is that self-important *"sput! - sput!"* comes from a strong motorcycle, and it's coming from the west, from the desert above the cliff-face – the desert Ray and I were setting out to cross when I told him about this. A man doesn't come that way unless he's got a reason, and a pretty good one, too.

So I walk out of the shack, out to where I can see the top of the cliff, and the noise gets closer. I look up but still can't see nothing. Then I hear the motor stop, with a noise like a tired sigh, and the snap of a kick-stand.

A second or two later, a head peeks over the cliff, looking down at me. Can't make out much about it that far away.

I wave.

The head jerks, like it wanted to pull back out of sight, but it sees that I seen it. An arm comes out and it waves back at me, then the whole man stands up and starts picking his way down the footpath that runs down the cliff to the mine. And he's moving stiff, like he's been some time in the saddle.

As he comes down, I can see he's a skinny kind of guy, not a big man, but he carries himself like he thinks maybe he ought to try looking like one, and for all I know then, maybe he's right. He's wearing khaki that isn't quite a uniform but don't miss it by much, with a knapsack on his back and a leather motorcycle helmet, pushed back on his head with the eye-goggles dangling down to one side. I don't see no gun on his hip, so I don't bother to go back inside for the Harrington.

No, I wait till he gets down the foot path, and then I see as he comes up to me; he's wearing a shoulder rig with a German Mauser: one of those they modified with a long barrel and a folding stock, like a short rifle or something, and where he carries it, he can pull it out pretty quick if he sets his mind to that.

Well, nothing I could do about it right then. I just stand there while he walks up to me and croaks out:

"*Bitte?*"

He points past me to the pump out by the bunkhouse, and I wave him to it. Doesn't take him long to get there and when he does, he starts jacking the handle. Soon as there's water, he pulls off his motorcycle gauntlets and holds his hands under. Rubs it over his face, fills the tin cup hanging on a chain there, drinks, spits to clear the dust from his mouth, then drinks again. Deep.

Finally, he turns to me.

"*K-k-anke*," he phlegms, clears his throat, and manages, "*Danke*."

"Take some more."

He does, and thanks me again, and I figure a good-mannered man like him, maybe he didn't mean to hide up there when I spotted him. Yeah, and maybe that long gun was just for shooting rabbits. Finally, he straightens up, looks around. Says something to himself in German.

"I beg pardon?" I say.

He looks at me like he'd come to my door selling something.

"I didn't quite catch what you said there," I smile friendly-like. "My name's Culley."

"Yes," he nods, "You are Culley. You own this, *Yah*?" He sweeps a hand at the rocky nothing all around.

"I run it, yeah."

"A mine, you run," He looks doubtful, kind of, at the smooth packed-earth road running up the gravel slope. The drainage ditch. The undisturbed spur road leading here from the highway. "Yet there gives no digging?"

"That's right." Nice of him to take an interest. "The plan was to get silver out of all this gravel. But they run out of money, the folks that own this place."

"No money?" He looks sad to hear it. And I mean that. Like he wished he could do something to ease my troubles. And then he starts walking around the place, sees the run-down sheds and jerry-rig buildings that used to be a going concern. "Your American economy, they say it is weak."

He says that while he's looking around, and it's funny, kind of like he doesn't want me to see how close he's looking the place over. Finally, he walks to the edge of the packed-dirt road and kicks at the gravel. "From this you get silver?"

I tell him a little about pouring acid on the rocks, and he nods approval.

"It is good," he says, "Science to unlock the treasures of Earth. A German idea."

Well, not hardly. Back in Virginia City, they used to get the same effect pouring bitterroot tea over low-grade. But I don't want to be disagreeable, not when we're getting along so good. I just say, "Smart thinking all right. Only I got to pack it all up and move on. Say, you got room for a passenger on that bike?"

He looks at me like he's going to say, *Yeah, hop on*, but then his face clouds up all thoughtful-like. And it stays that way a time. Finally, he asks, "No one comes here never?"

"Hardly never."

"No one comes yesterday?"

"No one comes the last week or so," I can feel my patience running kind of thin. "You lose a friend or something?"

He pushes the question around in his brain a minute, like it was heavy furniture, and I wonder if this guy's just slow-thinking or if something in my social life is really important to him, and finally, he answers:

"I must you this tell : It is the duty of a good German the others of the world less fortunate to help. And so, I would help you from this place to move. Yet I have also another duty. There is taken property of the German people, and-" he stops himself like he was going to talk more about this property of the German people but remembered not to. He finishes with, "-and to recover this may lead me into the way of some harm. I cannot put you also into the way of such harm. If my duty permits I shall to this return and provide you from this place to move."

"Well, I ain't talking about a long ride—" I start.

"It can do not do," His mind looks pretty well made up, and I figure a mind moves like his don't get changed real often so I give it up.

But he goes on, "Yet for you is this," and he unslings his knapsack. Pulls out two cans of peaches and gives them to me like Santy Claus at Christmas and I swear he almost pats my little head.

"There is no one else come here?" Like he's asking if I was a good boy, "Not for times?"

"Not for more'n a month."

"*Danke.*"

You see some funny sights in the desert, but probably not many like the look on my face while I watch that little

German climb up the footpath to the top of the cliff and ride off on his big motorcycle.

And me wondering about the ring on his finger – noticed it when he handed me the peaches—the ring with the death-head and swastika.

It didn't take long to tell Ray all this; we'd just got to the top of the cliff face when I got to the part about the ring, and he turned and looked close at me.

"A death-head? Over a swastika?" he asked.

"Sound like someone you know?"

"*Mijnheer* Ryckman told me once about a gang in Berlin called *Schutzstaffel*. That was their emblem: death-head and swastika. He seemed to think they were kind of a nasty bunch. Tough, I mean."

"Well, this one didn't seem like nothing special."

"That was his point: Ryckman said these men who wore the death-head didn't always strut around looking big, not like the goons in brown shirts, but..." he looked around for the right words a minute, "...well, according to him, if the Nazis want to do something really unpleasant—and they want it done right the first time—that's who does it for them."

"These guys who wear the death-head-and-swastika you mean? They do the hard parts?"

"The mean parts. That's what *Mijnheer* Ryckman said."

I thought that over some. Remembered how easy that little German went up and down the steep footpath me and Ray had just toiled up. How he wore that over-size Mauser so's I didn't see it till he got up close.

"And what's that word they call themselves?"

"*Schutzstaffel*. That's the proper name. But everyone just calls them the SS."

CHAPTER 10

Like I say, soon as it got dark enough, we picked our way up the cliff face and started out across the desert towards 'Nada, and I should tell you something about walking across the desert.

Well I didn't like it much.

The walk, I mean it wasn't one of these things like you see in the movies, where folks crawl across the sand with their tongues hanging out while buzzards circle overhead. We never even come close to dying, Ray and me, because if you know what you're doing and you don't run into any real bad luck, crossing the desert's no more dangerous than walking through Chinatown after dark with a gold watch and chain. But it was a hard trip; harder than I figured on, and maybe if I'd known just how rough it was going to be, I would have thought twice about just staying put and facing the Serrano Brothers back at Old Pesos.

The desert can be pretty to look at sometimes. The wind sand-blasts some of the rocks into funny shapes, with colored layers of granite, basalt, porphyry, and quartzite. Yellow sand twists across it in patterns set by the breeze, always changing. With a clear blue sky and bright sun, the sheer color of it can hit your eyes like a field of flowers and take the breath right out of you.

But this stretch of the Great Salad Desert was just hard-baked clay, brown dust, and heat.

Plant-wise, there were the usual cactuses: stubby prickly-pears, medium-size chollas, and rangy, long-armed saguaros. Also, some kind of trees: hard, stubborn-looking things I never knew the names of and just called 'em, "scrub-trees," with dusty, withered leaves, boney branches that gave no shade, and roots clear to hell. And some kind of shrub I called jack-brush, 'cause it seemed to fit.

Our route on the map was along what was left of an old wagon trail, mostly across a baked-clay plain, rocky stuff covered with sand and dust in places, with some softer stretches of barren soil, and there'd be a stretch of pure sand toward the end if we got that far. The way was broken up by outcrops of jagged rock, winding arroyos—long, jaggy trenches plowed across the ground by rogue thunderstorms every couple years—and way off in the distance, the cut-peak that was the nearest land-mark to 'Nada, which is where we was making for.

But you don't cross a desert by walking straight across it. You do it by going from one water-hole to the next, and that's the way the old wagon track ran. There was plenty of moon by the time we got started—it put everything in a silvery, hard-shadowed light that makes the desert almost pretty by night—so the trail was easy to see, but just to stay on the careful side I plotted a course to the water hole closest, checked the compass bearings against the old wagon ruts in the ground, and we started that way.

After about an hour's walk, we found a likely arroyo near a water hole with a lightning-blasted scrub-tree to serve as a marker, the branches twisted up like half of a crooked-cross shape, easy to remember—and that's where we stashed our bags of guns and books, under a jam-pile of jack-brush.

I noticed as we walked that Ray dragged his left leg some, but our pace was pretty well matched, and we made good time. Being night-time, it got cold, but we both wore long sleeves and thick-soled shoes. I had me a pair of old miner's boots I'd never used much and Ray wore those heavy work shoes you need to get along in the rough country. Ray also wore a raggy sombrero that would keep off the sun when it came, and I had an old floppy woven-straw thing that looked like I killed the Village Idiot and kept his hat. So, we was set to keep off the chill and the sun both.

We got in a good eight hours' walk by the time that sun showed up—seeing our way with coal oil lanterns after the moon set, 'cause it gets dark in the desert at night— and we walked another hour after sun-up till we found our water-hole by an outcrop of rock to shade us. I poked around the rocks with a stick, then poured oil from one of the lanterns in a big ring around where we planned to sleep out the day. There we settled in, ate tinned meat and crackers, washed down with plenty of water, and rested up good. The water was warm, cloudy, and awful hard; never really soaked into your mouth like good water does. But it was water and we drank our fill and then rinsed off the dust with it.

Soon as I'd drunk enough that my throat felt good for talking, I thanked Ray for saving those books. He just nodded and said, "You think the Serrano brothers will come after us?"

"Not going to worry about it. Hell, for all I know, that German's out here someplace, with his long gun and his peaches. I reckon, though, they'll figure it's just too much trouble to chase after us. And I told Paco I'd be back—in the note I left on the windshield. Mean to keep that promise, too."

Ray peered out from our shady spot, back across the miles of bright flat nothing we'd come over.

"Not much we could do about it if they did decide to come after us anyway."

"Not out here in all this open."

Out in the sun, a funny-looking lizard was standing still as a rock, maybe twenty yards off the other side of the waterhole, taking in the conversation maybe, studying the situation and sniffing the air. Wondering what was different about the place this morning, I guess. Here in the shade, Ray said, "Those books back there. Maybe I'll read them read someday." He chewed on a cracker, slowly, to get all the good out of it. "Just as soon as we take care of this little matter."

I was getting used to how when Ray smiled, the scar next to his mouth deepened, and gave him a sneaky, twisted look. I knew by then it was just a look, but it sure was ugly enough to put off a stranger.

Out in the sun, that lizard I'd been watching had just about decided to come down to the water hole. There was another one a ways behind him, looking things over for himself. It occurred to me I might be getting sleepy, but I was restless too, kind of, and Ray was saying something,

"*Mijnheer* Ryckman sure must have loved her."

"His wife you mean?"

"Yeah, his wife. He sure must have loved her to take on a job like this."

"Yeah, I guess so."

"What kind of thing you think it is, to make a man give up everything, his family, his home—even his life—just to care for a woman?"

"A man's feelings can do funny things with him," I sighed. His talk had got my attention off the lizards and half woke me up again. "I just guess a thing like that's hard to figure."

"You ever had a woman like that?" Ray finished eating and now he took off his boots and socks while he talked. He rinsed his socks out in the fresh water from his canteen, then got a can of foot-powder from his pocket and sprinkled it liberally in his boots. "Someone important to you like that?"

"Almost did," I said, "It might've turned out like that anyway. Hell, I don't know; a man can bide his time till his time runs out, I guess,"

I shifted around on the hard, shady ground and tried to get comfortable. "Met a girl in college a few years back, and we got kind of attached one to another. I guess most of the guys in school, they thought she was small and kind of mousy-looking, but I ... well, I thought she was sort of pretty. And she had a way about her, I don't know what exactly but..."

Out in the sun, the two lizards moved down towards the water hole in short, sudden skitters. But I wasn't watching them, I was thinking of back when...

"But Hell, back then I was just a guy pushing thirty with a shady past, no job, and slim prospects—pretty much what I am now, come to think on it, except now I'm pushing forty: just older, that's all. And if a man wants to marry a woman, he ought to be able to keep her—provide for her, you know?"

"That's what people say."

"When old man Kurtz hired me to rekindle Old Pesos Mine, I thought maybe I'd ask her to marry me. And I think she would have. But then I figured it better to work a while and put some money back. We agreed she'd wait some for me. Had no way knowing I'd be nigh onto seven years down here and nothing to show for it."

"What happened with her?"

"Could be she's still up Kansas City way looking for me to come calling with my pockets full of silver. Doubtful, though. We wrote a lot at first when I first come down here. She said in a letter once maybe she could come down, said she grew tired waiting. I almost went ahead and asked her to. But the Mail got kind of spotty along about that time, and I guess we let it pass. By then we both saw I wasn't getting out of here anytime soon, and wouldn't have much to show for it when I did. I couldn't go back to her that way. And things have been kind of unsettled since hard times come, I hear. Folks moving around just to get work, I don't even know she's still there. The last letter she said she'd pray for me, but it don't look to have done much good."

Ray offered me the can of foot powder, and I used it likewise, glad to be hooked up with a man who knew to take care of his feet on a walk like this. We laid our old socks in the Sun to dry, put on clean ones, and stretched out again in the shade. Out in the sun, the lizards I seen earlier had just about made it down to the water hole, but they stopped dead-still till Ray and I quit moving again.

"Kind of shy, I guess," Ray said, "The lizards, I mean."

He didn't miss much, this boy.

At the water hole, both lizards were standing at the edge with their mouths right at the water, and I guessed they must be drinking, but they were still as rocks and their skin had turned the same color as the dirt around them.

"You been watching those creepies?" I asked.

"Some; getting hard to see them."

"Think you could take a shot and hit one this far off?"

"Maybe," he shrugged, and his Army .45 was in his hand and he was sighting down the barrel at the lizards.

It was that smooth: not sudden, jerky, or showy-fast; it was just his body rippled, and that big gun was lined up. The lizards hadn't even noticed.

"But that'd just be meanness, I guess." Ray put his side-arm back as natural as he'd pulled it out. "And besides, a dead lizard would bring the buzzards down on us, and buzzards are nasty, smelly things."

Maybe he had a point, but he'd got me to wondering where he'd learned to move like that. Didn't seem polite to ask right out, though, so I just said, "You'll excuse me asking, Ray, but you don't exactly talk like a Mexican truck driver."

"I'm American as you are," he said, a trace proud of it, "Born in Arizona. Father was Mexican, mother was full-blood Navajo. She taught school on a reservation."

"She must have give you some good education."

"She gave me a passion for books, anyway."

"She did a good job. Was your dad an educated man too?"

"He was a mechanic. He read sometimes, but not for the pleasure of it. He was always proud of my reading, though. He ran a garage for a while, fixing cars, and I helped out when I was old enough." Ray stretched his legs out and half-laid back. "But when Mother died, he seemed to lose interest and let the business go."

"Must have hit him hard."

"Well, he sure let the business go. We lost the house, and next thing I knew, all we owned was a war-surplus ambulance, and we were working for the Hudders."

"Who-ders?"

"Hudders: Dutch folks, trying their luck in Nevada. Don't ask me how or why they came to settle out there, but Mister. Hudder had a nice farm and he got along well with Father -" he turned to me. "You know, it's funny how things turn out. The house was full of books: all of them in Dutch. Well, one day a wasp stung Mr. Hudder, he swung his scythe wide, and it hit me in the face."

He fingered the scar by his mouth.

"It got infected. I lay in bed a month and more. With nothing to do and all those books about, I started trying to read them, and Mrs. Hudder helped me learn the language. And speaking Dutch is how I came to be hired by the late *Mijnheer* Ryckman. If it hadn't been for that wasp stinging old man Hudder..."

"...You wouldn't be sitting here in the desert trying to rescue a half-ton of Gold."

"Funny, eh?"

"I could laugh out loud and spill my tea. Remind me if I don't get to it right away."

I looked out by the water hole, but now I couldn't see either one of the lizards; they'd either gone while I wasn't watching or blended in with the color of the ground well enough I couldn't see them. I blinked to focus my eyes. Ray and me both had been up for near onto two days now, and some of it had been hard work. The only thing keeping us going right now was the jolt a man gets from getting shot at. Or shooting back.

Just then I saw a shadow out on the dry plain beyond the water hole. Just a small dark thing moving fast across the ground. My eye was drawn to the edge of the water, and I just *just* saw a little wrinkle-movement over the rocks; the lizards had seen that shadow too, or sensed it some way and—

—*Whup!*

There was a quick swoop of feathers, a hawk swung down from on high, grabbed a lizard, killed it in its talons— even in that flash-second we saw that bird's claws go bright red with blood—and flew away, just that quick, while Ray and me watched. The other lizard, his lucky friend, had clear vanished.

"Guess that's how it is," I said, "one gets his drink and gets away, one don't."

"No more sense to it than that?"

"Not so as I can see it."

I was getting tired. Come to that, we were both pretty worn down anyway. Ray squinted out toward where the lizard had just vanished and said, "Well, sleep well, Culley."

"You too, Ray."

I closed my eyes, but the sun out there beyond our shade was so bright now it seemed I could see the red back of my eyelids. See through them, just about. I tried to look through my eyelids at the water hole, and thought about the two lizards.

Ray had almost shot one but then decided not to. Hadn't done the lizard any good, though, because the hawk got him. But maybe the hawk hadn't got the one he would've shot, maybe he got the other one. By sparing the one, he'd set the other one up to get killed. Or maybe it was the first lizard that had been marked for dying today all along, and when Ray didn't kill him, the hawk came down and did it. Then it struck me I must be asleep. Because I was dreaming about all that Gold back in the mine shaft at Old Pesos.

And how I could get my pockets full of it.

CHAPTER 11

It was maybe six or eight hours later when the heat woke us up. I had a dream I was in a burning house and my foot was on fire, and I woke up and found out I was only half right: the shade we were in had shifted while we slept and now my right foot was out in the sun, damn-near burning.

I haven't talked much about the heat so far, because if you live in the desert you get used to it. Like a blind man gets used to dark. But I'm here to tell you the heat was hot. Sucked the breath right out of you and beat you down like a big slapping hand. Ray and I were still in the shade, but my foot was out in the sun, and it felt like I'd stuck it in a fireplace. Good job I had my socks on, or I might have burned it too bad to walk.

I pulled back in the shade, of course, but that didn't make things any cooler. Ray was awake too. It was too hot to sleep. Too hot to lay still, even. Ray said he'd seen cattle in heat like this go mad and run across the plain till they fell over dead. I said I didn't much want to do that.

"There's only two-three hours of daylight left," I said, "Guess we might as well head out. Unless you've got plans?"

"Nothing too pressing," Ray smiled his ugly face-twisting smile, and I found I was getting used to it. We opened another can of meat and some crackers, washed it down good from the water hole, filled our canteens and bellies, straining the cloudy water through handkerchiefs. I checked the map and the wagon track, then took a sighting toward the next water hole.

"Maybe fifteen miles out that way." I checked my compass bearings against the angle of shadows thrown by the cactus and the direction of the sun, so we'd know if the trail went off from the right direction. "Ready?"

"I guess," Ray rubbed a thumb thoughtfully up the stubble on his cheek, like he wanted to say something, almost had to say it. But he just slung his canteen around his neck and we started out walking across the long shadows, away from the water hole, out towards the sunset. Where there were no shadows.

I already said it was hot. Well, I could say it again. I could write "Hot" clear down the page and it still wouldn't put it across. And let me tell you about drinking water in the desert: don't try to save it up too much. You want to save a little, just so you can think about having it if you need it, but otherwise just go ahead and drink it when you want it. There's men found dead in the sand with full canteens right next to them; so scared of running out of water they waited too long to drink, and fried their brains I guess, or maybe got too weak. Ray felt the same as me about this, so we drank plenty right off. Yeah, we had long sleeves and big hats to keep the sun off, but it was still damn-awful hot. Damn awful hot.

We'd been going about an hour, and the Sun was pretty near down to the horizon when Ray took a drink of water and cleared his throat. "We were talking about Religion back there at the mine."

"Was we?"

"*Mijnheer* Ryckman and how he turned Jewish; You think he went to Heaven anyway? In spite of being Jewish?"

"Seems like he should have. Maybe the Jews are right and there ain't any Christ. But if there is, I hear He's the forgiving sort, and a guy like Ryckman dies trying to make his wife proud of him, he ought to get to Heaven easy enough."

"Christ—if there is Christ—would forgive him turning Jewish?"

"I can't speak for Jesus." I put my canteen to my lips and took a long pull. "We never been close, me and Him. But that's what they say. He forgives all of it. Everything."

"I think He forgives most things." Ray took another short sip. "Almost everything, as you say. But there might be some things He can't wave his hand and make it all right—I mean there's some things you do and you can't just say 'I'm sorry' and get forgiven."

"Like what for instance?"

"Killing, sometimes."

"Sometimes?" The conversation was slowing us down some and I knew I ought to pick up the pace, but it seemed like Ray wanted to say this, and I ought to hear it. "Some kinds of killing, I'm guessing."

"Killing a child. Or rape. You'd have to be truly penitent for Him to forgive violating a woman," Ray ran his tongue around his mouth, trying to soak up whatever was left of that swallow he took. "Or breaking a promise to a dying man."

That damn near stopped me in my tracks. Kept walking, though.

"Could be," I said carefully. "So?"

"I'm thinking that if breaking a promise to a dying man is an unpardonable sin, then perhaps..." He chewed on it a minute, then, "Perhaps keeping such a promise—no matter how hard it is—perhaps keeping such a promise may wipe out another such sin. Do you think?"

I looked over at him. Neither one of us broke stride. Then, "The way you put it makes sense," I said, "And if I was Christ maybe that's how I'd work things out. But listen, Ray: if you're figuring on getting into Heaven by delivering Ryckman's Gold, you're apt to get disappointed. We got some long odds headed our way, and if we get to the end of it—" I wanted to tell him how I'd felt when I saw all that Gold, the nice things it could mean for me, and I wanted to mention that maybe we didn't need to take the whole thing back to the Dutchman's daddy-in-law if we ever got that far, which didn't look likely.

Then, all of a sudden, I remembered something. Don't know why it flashed into my mind just then, but I recalled taking a test back in college, and the professor hands me back my grade, and on the bottom of it he wrote,

"HAMLET, Mr. Culley, is about a great task being laid upon a soul unequal to it. A description, I fear, which applies to you as well."

I wondered if there was some way to get across to Ray what I was thinking.

"You're an educated man," I said, "Ever read a book called HAMLET?"

"I saw it as a play once. I sort of liked it. I don't remember anything in it about crossing a desert, though."

"No, but everybody dies at the end. All of them. Dead as crackers. And that could be us. In this game, we ain't no more than a pair of deuces in a whole deck full of face cards." I let him think on that while I took a short pull on my canteen, just enough to wet my lips. "We got the Serrano brothers back there behind us, the desert here in front, and a peach-packin' Nazi out there somewhere. If this is your plan on getting to Heaven—"

I didn't finish the thought. Didn't need to, and my mouth was getting too dry to waste words. Ray just nodded and I saw he understood, even if he wasn't real happy over it.

Now mind you, at that time—right then—I hadn't full made up my mind to take as much of that Gold as I could and get away with it. But I knew me pretty well, and I was pretty sure I couldn't be trusted with a whole lot of money, prom-ise-to-a-dying-man or not. But I didn't want to tell Ray that one of the things standing in his way to Heaven might be me. Nossir, no sense in bringing that up right then at all.

No sense doing anything but walking.

CHAPTER 12

The two of us kept an even pace with each other, but it was slower today, and I saw Ray was dragging his other leg now. Might be muscles seizing up with dehydration. Or maybe not; a man drives a truck for a living, his legs get funny sometimes.

After a while the sun went down and it cooled off some, but by then we were too tired to appreciate it. When it got too dark to walk, we sat down and waited for the Moon to come up so we could see to get going again, and while we waited we stretched out on the warm, hard ground and shared the last can of meat between us. I couldn't taste it much, and what I did taste was salty and greasy-like, but it felt good to have something in my mouth besides dust for a change.

"Culley?" Sitting there, it was too dark to see Ray's face when he talked but I heard him take a short swig of water and hold it in his mouth awhile before going on, "We may not feel like talking much later on, but you got me curious. Forgive me, but you don't talk much like a College man, do you?"

"I used to run some with low company," I said.

And I started telling him about myself: son of a Southern Ohio dirt farmer. School and a knack for science. Come 1917, America entered the Great War, the war to end all wars, and I was just old enough and big enough to lie about my age, join the Army and get over there in time for the Last Big Push, the final charge that would wipe out the whole damn German Army.

Yeah, I was there for it, the Last Big Push. And the one after that. And the one after that. And the next couple dozen, too.

"Time I got back," I was saying, "There weren't a lot of good jobs around, so I went to college for an Engineering Degree. That's where I learned mining and Spanish, in college, that is. Worked my way through school running hooch for a man named Seamus Feeney in Kansas City."

"Dangerous work?"

"Not the way I did it," I took a swig of water myself. "Feeney never sent one man on a job when he could send three. And he made sure if you worked for him, you carried heat and knew how to use it. 'I don't care what you shoot,' he'd say 'but you will by God hit what you shoot at and nothing else. The Good Lord calls it a sin to waste bullets, and I won't have any man of mine leave one lying around where it's not wanted to go.'"

"Mr. Feeney sounds like a good man to work for."

"He was, but it was just a job to me. Some guys do work like that, it gets to be a habit, kind of, a way of life with them. You've heard the expression 'Life of Crime?' Some men take it serious, but I was just working my way through college; like washing dishes or something. After a while I got my degree and found honest work—while it lasted."

No point telling Ray how Seamus Feeney came to meet his end with a bullet from his own gun stuck in his brains. No one ever figured out who put it there anyway, and I sure wasn't telling.

"Seems there are quite a few men who fought in the war, planned a career, then had it fall out from under them back in '29," Ray's voice was getting a little raspy and I heard him shake his canteen, trying to calculate if he should take another swallow. He decided not to.

"I guess so." My mouth was getting dry too, despite the drink I just had. I hefted my canteen, listened to the water in it, and figured to wait a bit for the next one myself. "But not many of them know how to pull Gold out of a silver mine."

Ray tried to laugh at that but his throat was too dry. Mine was getting that way too, but by now the moon had come up enough to see, so we made each other get up and start walking again. I noticed Ray's limp was a little worse, but he was still keeping good pace with me. And I guess my throat was too dry to tell Ray the rest of that story about my Kansas City days. Or maybe I just didn't want him on his guard around me.

There's not much water in the desert. Maybe you heard about that already. But I said earlier there's water that comes out in the desert at night, and there is—they call them night rivers. Here's how it works: those scrub trees with roots clear to Hell suck up water from aquifers under the ground—in the daytime that is. But after dark, they shut down, and the water they were using comes to the surface and flows in small-size trickles. Then at dawn, the trees start sucking up water again, and the first rays of the sun evaporate any moisture that didn't sink through the sand. And the night rivers disappear.

That's what someone told me, anyway. But where we were walking, there weren't any scrub trees; just some jack-brush that looked ready to crumble to dust. I started thinking real serious about the water hole we were headed to.

If there's water anywhere around, it's not hard to find, provided you have a general idea and know what to look for. The moon was good again tonight, and as we followed the old wagon track and got closer to the spot marked on the map, I started looking to see more old wheel marks, animal signs, and that kind of thing. Once I spotted the hard-baked ruts of another old wagon track joining this one, the path was easy to follow. We were headed the right way.

Then I saw the prairie dog skeleton shining white in the moonlight. It was lying on the hard ground, complete. Picked clean by ants, but not buried in the dust yet. It was fairly recent. And it was facing us.

I don't know if Ray saw it, or understood it if he did: some prairie dog, coming this way—away from the water hole—had stopped there and died. Maybe of thirst, or maybe from poison water.

I told myself one skeleton doesn't make a bad water hole, and we kept walking. Nothing much else to do. After a while, we passed another skeleton: something bigger, a coyote maybe, smooth and whole. And facing our way.

By the time we got to where the water hole used to be, bones were fairly common, and I knew with nothing being said Ray could tell what they meant. There, where we were hoping for water, was just a shallow depression with a rough almost-circle of bones around it—none human, but plenty of animals. Near the middle of the circle there was a withered tree of some kind and under the tree a little patch of coarse, dead, brown-green grass.

No water though.

We didn't say a word to each other, just picked the biggest bones we could find and started digging up the ground under the coarse grass. If a bone snapped, we got another. There were plenty.

After a while, we found mud and sucked on it some. Made us strong enough to dig again, and this time we found muddy water. I tried to strain it through a handkerchief, but it was too thick. We just put what we could in our canteens and hoped it would settle.

We scooped out a little pocket in the bottom of our diggings, and about every fifteen minutes it would fill with a mouthful of mud-water, and we took turns drinking it. Finally, Ray's throat got wet enough to say, "How far to 'Nada?"

I checked the position of the setting moon against my compass bearing. If I was right, the moon was just now disappearing a shade to the right of our direction of travel. And I better be right. I lit our last match and double-checked the map.

"Ten miles. Fifteen, maybe."

The match went out just the same time the moon set, leaving us in dark, but off to the east, the sky was already showing some light, so it wouldn't be long till the sun come up again. And brought the heat with it.

"All right." Ray's voice was hoarse from the mud-water, but he made himself talk, so I figured it must be important. "Before we go, there's this you should know: I killed a man last year. In 'Nada, the place we're going. They never put a warrant out on me, but when we get there, there are those in 'Nada who would nail me to a wall. And you alongside me, if they think we're friends."

I chewed on that for a time.

"No help for it," I said after a while, "We got no place else to go and nothing else to do. Maybe we get there, you can lay up outside town or something till I get help. We'll make do."

"Are you sure?"

"I don't much want to cross this last stretch alone." Off to the East it was getting light, pretty near good enough to see by, and I made myself get up. "If it comes to worst, I'll just say I brung you in for Bounty and help them shoot you."

He grinned and got up himself. "Let's go then."

The sky turned red with full sunrise all to once, and we could see the way clear. Because it was flat. And empty. No trees, no rocks, no shade. No place to hide from the sun that was coming. And no sense waiting here.

"Looks easy," one of us said.

CHAPTER 13

We'd been walking about an hour and covered maybe two miles by the time the sun came full up and it commenced to get hot. That slowed us down some, and we didn't need slowing down. The muscles were starting to cramp up from dehydration, getting us clumsy-moving, like a couple of drunks just starting to stagger. But we kept walking.

Ray and I didn't want to lose each other, but it was too much work to stop and turn every so often. Without saying it, we worked out a rhythm. I'd pass him and walk in front awhile, then I'd slow up and he'd pass me and walk in front awhile, then he'd slow up and I'd pass him and walk in front awhile, then I'd slow up…

It came back to me what Ray said about cows running mad in the heat, and I could see where they had a point. The heat does that to you. That and more. When there's nothing to do but walk, that gets to be all you can think: Walk. Your mind gets slow and gummed-up and you turn stupid with just walk… walk…

When the sun got high enough, the mirages started showing up. Which was another reason I didn't like to walk the desert in full daylight: the mirages, I mean.

Now a mirage is nothing but a reflection of the sky, caused by the hot air of the desert floor when it bounces off the cooler air high-up and makes kind of a mirror-effect that looks just like a pool of water there on the ground. Anyone who's driven the highway on a hot summer day has seen mirages: the odd-shaped, shiny things that shimmer in the distance and look a little like water till they shift away when you get close.

That's when you're driving. When you're walking, bent over by the heat and moving slow, the mirage doesn't shift away so fast; seems like it's always out there, just in front of you, or off to one side, and if you think about it much, you can almost smell the water, but if you're smart you know it's not really out there. You ignore it. And keep walking.

I was smart enough to know that, and so was Ray, but I can tell you it still got on my nerves. Maybe it wasn't bad enough, the desert being hot and miserable like it was, but now it was getting mean, too. Laughing at us for what we couldn't have.

Like I say, it got on my nerves some, but we kept going, and after a couple hours the sun got low and the mirages disappeared. And we kept walking.

Up in the distance, I saw a spot on the ground: nothing big, just a rock maybe a foot across, sticking up there a ways in front. There was something under the shadow of it, tan and funny-shaped. Couldn't think what it could be, but

I kept walking toward it. As we got closer, I saw it might be a snake, but I never thought to walk around it.

That's how much the sun makes you stupid. I just saw myself walking closer and closer to the snake and knew I was going to step on it, and couldn't make myself stop or turn aside. I felt my tall miner's boot squash it, felt it twist and writhe under me, heard the hiss-warning, felt the fangs hit harmlessly on my boot and bounce back, and the whole thing made no more impression than a bug hits your windshield.

Somewhere I remember thinking I just damn-near died of snake-bite, and somewhere else in my head I wondered if that would be better or worse than going on walking like this.

About that time the ground got sandy, then more sandy, then all sand, moving underfoot, slowing us up even more, and I started listening to it.

The sand makes a sound: Millions, maybe millions-of-millions of grains of sand shifting, sliding over each other, falling, moving, blowing, and settling again. Makes a sound like someone whispering in your ear, and now and then you almost make out what it's saying.

Whisper. Walk. *Whisper.* Walk. *Whisper.* Walk.

Close to sunset, we were maybe only a few miles out from 'Nada, but we had no way of knowing that. All we knew was that we might not make it. Just maybe weren't going to do it.

We were walking west, and the setting sun was so bright it almost closed my eyes. Now the temperature rose past a hundred, and each breath was a hot, hateful, lung-scorching effort that just seemed like too much trouble. And all the time the sand kept murmuring to me. In a loud stage-whisper now, but I still couldn't make out the words.

Maybe, I thought, *maybe if I put my ear to the ground, I'll understand.*

My knees gave out and I hit the ground, so tired by then it felt good. Laid out on the sand, I turned my ear to the ground and listened.

The sand was whispering to me. And I understood it.

I opened my eyes and saw what the sand was telling me. I was lying in a long, shallow depression, and about a half-mile away, up a small rise, I could just see the tops of a couple scrub-trees. No rocks, no shade to get under, and no, no water.

But the sand kept whispering.

Ray caught up to me then, dragging his one leg worse than ever, and he made as if to get me up again, and I shook my head No. He didn't have the strength for it anyway. At first, he thought I was taking a rest or had laid down to die—which amounted to the same thing. Neither one of us could talk, but I looked at him, and some way I made him understand we had to stay here to save our lives. He nodded and sank to his knees as the sun set, and we both collapsed there in the shallow ditch.

It was full dark for about an hour when I felt the first cool, wet water ooze up under my back.

Not long after that, I heard the sound of it, just a flicker, not a flow. But not much later I got the strength to turn over and touch my lips in the narrow, trickling night river we were lying in, there in the desert.

"How?" Soon as his lips could move enough to talk, Ray asked me this, he asked, "How did you know to stop here?" he took another drink of the cold trickling water. "How did you know it would come up here?"

Maybe I learned it back in college, then forgot I knew it—I slept through a lot of classes on Hydrology back then. Or maybe the Geology I learned put it somewhere in the back of my head that a long, shallow depression like we were in had to be the bed of a stream. Hell, I might've half-heard it in a bar, standing next to a drunken prospector. I probably had a picture of it back in my mind somewhere and knew how to look for a night river. That was probably what made me stop there, where I did.

But right then I was too tired and too glad to be alive to make up lies. I just said, "The sand told me. Whispered it to me."

And Ray nodded he understood.

CHAPTER 14

By eight or nine that night we were pretty near human again. The water saved our lives, but it didn't do much else; we were still too whipped to talk much, and we had just about enough strength to walk into 'Nada in the last of the moonlight. Some way, Ray croaked out that there was a *cantina* in town, and it would be dim-lit enough we could both get inside, and Ray could find a dark corner while I got us food and drink. And it seemed like a good idea for me to pretend I didn't speak Spanish. That's about as much deep thought as we could manage. Any idea about Ray holing up outside of town was all forgot about.

Ray led me into town, and there wasn't much to it: one street in the whole place, and it was pretty much rolled up for the night when we staggered in.

They don't make towns like 'Nada anymore, and that's a good idea, too. This Main Street we come walking up was a wide, straggly thing, heading up from the edge of the desert where we come from to the foothills beyond us. There were maybe twenty-or-so buildings along it, some facing the road, some backing up to it and some just set where they pleased.

Down the middle of the street, there was an open sewer with a smell likely to chase a hungry buzzard off a dead buffalo, trickling slowly downhill to no place special. Every few yards or so the trickle hit a pothole and filled it up, and wherever that happened, two or three skinny pigs had set up their camp there, wallowing in it and eating whatever came their way. Kind of put me off eating pork, it did. Leastways from that part of the country.

"It was a good town," Ray managed, "A few years back. A good town, not some adobe village."

I saw the hulking shadow of some big factory-looking building at the far end of town, but no lights or anything coming from it, no trucks or wagons close by. Most of the rest of 'Nada was gray cinder block places with tin roofs. A few nicer ones were brick—there was a brick Jail, I recall—and some older places were adobe, with thatch roofs.

"Looks like it maybe seen better days," I pushed the words out of my hoarse throat.

And it sure looked run-down now, with busted windows, open doorways, and a general feel of Moved Out. There was no electricity in 'Nada, and now the moon had set it turned pretty dark, and I was glad to have Ray to guide me. Probably just as well the town was so quiet when we got there because the way we looked and the way we walked would have got some attention from anyone out and about. But there was no one around and no lights except one open doorway that seemed not quite as dark as the others. That had to be the *cantina*.

Over the door was a faded sign, PALACIO. Ray slipped in and moved straight to the darkest corner while I made it to the bar and told the skinny old man behind it—in English—I wanted four bottles of soda pop and anything to eat. Which is what I got.

I would've rather got beer, but when you're dried out like we were, even a little bit of alcohol can knock you on your ass. The old man kept his bottles of soda pop in a tub of water to make it look like they were cool, with the water dripping off the sides. They weren't cool at all, but the soda pop was foamy and smooth and that was just fine. I carried four bottles of it and a plate of something back to the corner where Ray had planted himself and took a short pull on the soda. Held it in my mouth and let it soak out the dust before I washed it down my throat.

Then there was the food. Whatever we were eating tasted like some desert critter got clubbed to death and then they melted cheese on it, but it fit in my mouth, mostly, and the drink helped it go down. When we finished, I went back up to the bar for more, and now I wasn't so near death, I figured a couple beers might be safe. Also got a chance to look around.

It was the kind of place where you slap a *centavo* on the bar and a scorpion comes out and dances on the floor. A real family place. Hard-packed dirt floor, with three adobe walls, and the fourth, where we sat, opened onto something that smelled like a stable. Close by us, down at that end, a few chickens slept in the rafters, and I think maybe there was a pig nesting in one corner. Too dark to say for sure, though.

The only light was from lanterns hung at the bar and over some of the tables. Someone had cut apart big tin cans, polished the insides, and fixed them over the lanterns to reflect the light down and make the most of it. Likewise, the walls were white-washed clean and shiny so you could see around pretty good.

There was, like I say, a few lanterns hanging around the room, mostly not-lighted, which suited us fine. Three or four mixed-bag tables and maybe a dozen chairs, a kitchen back of the bar, and what looked like a couple rooms to one side. That was the Palacio.

Two men were playing cards under one of the lights, dealing those big, bright-colored Mexican playing cards and using bottle caps for poker chips. Or maybe they were playing for bottle caps, I don't know. There had been a third man at the bar when we came in, a short fellow in a fancy jacket, but he must've gone to the outhouse or something. A wind-up gramophone behind the bar, turned way down, was scratching out a familiar song—a catchy thing, popular right then, something about a crying woman. So soft you could hardly hear it.

The door was some wider than in a house, but not wide enough to pass two men at once. The bar was kind of low for a bar—just at waist level—but clean and solid-built. So was the skinny old guy behind it: short gray beard, long gray hair, deep tanned skin, creased like a 'gator, with the same sleepy, patient eyes.

I thanked the old man—careful to speak just English—for his service, bought two beers, and asked was there a place to spend the night. He pointed at an open doorway off to one side and said it was five *centavos*. I pretended not to understand till he raised five fingers, then I put a Mexican quarter on the bar for the rooms and beer both.

When I got back to the table, Ray had his head down asleep. I set his beer in front of him and sat down.

There was someone else at the bar. I hadn't seen him come in, but he was leaning on that low bar there like he felt right at home. A big, rangy-looking fellow that's hard for me to tell about: his dark hair looked—not carefully barbered, but like it just naturally grew in neat. Likewise, the mustache under his long, broken nose, above his wide, good-natured mouth. Dressed in khaki that didn't look fancy but it fit him real good, the sleeves rolled up to show big, muscled arms.

He just relaxed there at the bar, never looking around, while the bartender brought him a Tequila. The old guy set the drink in front of this big fellow—along with a little bowl of salt and a tired-looking piece of lemon—then carefully brought out a chessboard, like he didn't want to disturb the pieces on it. They each made a couple moves, then a couple more. Then the big guy raised an eyebrow, laughed, dug into his pocket, and slapped a coin on the bar. The old man slipped it in his pocket, smiled, and went to pour another drink. While he did, the big man lazily turned our way and I saw something shiny pinned to his chest—and two German Luger pistols belted on his hips.

Now in the years from 1917 to 1930, there were probably more German guns in Mexico than in Germany. Those early Lugers weren't good weapons for indoor shooting— I never liked them, anyway—because they ejected the hot shell casing straight up, hard enough to bounce off a ceiling and hit the shooter in the head. Or roll down inside his shirt. But they were good-shooting guns, no argument about that. And it's not many men can walk around with that much artillery and not look kind of puny, but on this guy, they seemed part of him.

Part of the natural, easy-going stride as he came over to us.

I saw Ray still had his head down, but one hand had slipped down under the table, where his Army .45 was holstered, as the law-man came up and smiled gently down at him.

"You came back, old friend," he said softly, "I told Otilio you would."

Ray slowly turned his face up, just watched him while the big man watched him back, standing there easy-grinning. Ray's right hand still hung under the table.

"Well, you killer-of-boys." The big guy kept grinning down at Ray like he was discussing the weather with the mail-man, "Are you going to try it?"

All this was in Spanish, of course. I sat there pretending not to know any of it, just smiling like an idiot, which folks say I do pretty good. The big guy was focused on Ray, so this might be my chance to do something cute.

"Excuse me, sir," I said in English, "Do you know the way to Seattle?" I turned in my seat as I said it, fumbling my beer bottle with my left hand to keep him from seeing my right slip closer to my holster under the table, out of his sight. "Can that man tell me?"

I pointed past him with the beer bottle and half-rose, swinging into position to clout him upside the head with it while I pulled my gun and Ray pulled his.

That was the plan, anyway.

Didn't work out like that. Not at all.

Not quite sure what went wrong. Maybe neither one of us was at his best, after baking three days in the desert, but I never got my gun out and neither did Ray. Last I saw, the big man was just standing there grinning, his hands nowhere near me, and then somebody's big left fist—his, I think—come out of nowhere and flattened my face out while I was still trying to stand up.

Then there was just the pain of it, and me flying back to hit the wall behind us, and somewhere I felt him jerk the bottle from my hand and heard a dull *crack!* As he smashed it down across Ray's head.

I hit the wall back of me, and as I bounced off, I felt the big man's left fist again, slamming deep into my stomach.

I doubled over and he grabbed me by the hair and just plain threw me on the floor. Next thing I knew, I was face-down, the overturned table on top of me, and the point of a German Luger stuck in my ear. I strained an eye as far as I could and saw the big guy had nailed my head to the floor with his gun, still holding me down with it, while his other Luger was pushed up Ray's nose.

And I never even saw him move. He was that good.

So there I was, there on the floor, looking back over my life and wishing I'd learned some useful trade in school—anything but mining—while I braced myself for the shot I'd never hear. Then Ray saved both our lives. With one finger.

He raised that finger slow, like *"Just a minute, please,"* then reached -slowly- down to his pants leg. Raised the trouser cuff, reached under, real slow now, and I heard him peel tape off his calf.

There was a dull metal thud as a Gold Bar dropped on the floor.

"There's more," He whispered under the gun-barrel up his nose, "Half a ton of it. Out in the desert."

CHAPTER 15

S ometime later it occurred to me that all the time we were taking that God-awful walk across the desert, Ray must have been doing it with ten pounds of Gold taped to one leg—no wonder he was dragging some.

Right now, though, I was lying in a dark, wet, stinking cell, and the sound of him screaming in the next room kept me awake.

There were other voices, too: Milianos—the big lawman who'd taken us both down at once—was patiently asking Ray about the Gold. Ray was telling him there was lots more, but he'd have to deal us both in to get at it. There was another voice, deeper, but kind of thin and whiney, that called Ray a lying kid-killing son of a *gringo* whore, and there was a loud *slap-slap!* and Ray screamed at him and the voice screamed back and there was more slapping and screaming. Then Milianos asked where the Gold was again, and Ray answered he'd have to deal us both in to get at it... and more slapping and more screaming.

Kept me awake, like I say, and did a good job of it, too.

Milianos quieted things down after a while. "You wear on my patience." His voice was so gentle I could hardly hear it through the wall. "Perhaps I should leave Otilio here to work it out of you?"

"You leave him here alone with me," Ray answered just as gentle, "And bring back two men to carry out his fat carcass when you return. Because I will surely kill him."

There were another couple of slaps and more nasty talk from Otilio (I guess his name was; we never got formally introduced.) but when Milianos left, Otilio left with him. And they both came into my cell.

"*Buenas noches, Senor...?*" Milianos said it like he'd say Howdy to the barber.

"The name's Culley," I got up and talked in English, "And I think you may have made a mistake back there in the bar—"

"And I think you speak Mexican as well as I do," Milianos said in Spanish.

If you've got a God-given talent for something you should use it, so I just gave him a stupid look.

He never took his smiling eyes off me, just said in Spanish, "Kick his *cojones* off, Otilio."

There's a prize now for Best Actor, and right then I would've won it hands down if I had a better audience; just kept looking blank while Otilio came up and kicked me in the crotch.

Now this Otilio guy has a part in the story later on, so I better tell about him: He was trying to look like Milianos, but he missed it by a good half-mile. He was big, like Milianos, and he wore his clean mechanic coveralls something like Milianos wore his khaki uniform. He styled his hair the same as Milianos and even had his neat little mustache. But where Milianos' eyes were hard and penetrating, his were shifty and a little stupid. His chin was weak, and every so often he kept glancing at the boss to see was he doing good.

And right now, like I say, he did himself right proud kicking my family heirlooms while I tried to look stupider than he did.

When the toe of his boot came up I swayed forward just a mite, moved my legs together, half-catching his boot between my thighs, jumped up quick, screamed, and doubled over. Then I fell on the floor and curled up, whimpering something awful.

Looked just like I got kicked in the jewels, but all Otilio really done was graze my butt. I learned this trick from a German prisoner-of-war, but let me warn you if you want to try it sometime—it takes a little practice.

Anyhow, I rolled on the floor looking agonized and Milianos said, "I guess he really doesn't know Spanish."

"Stupid *gringo* bastard." Otilio kicked me in the ribs for being a stupid *gringo* bastard, and because he could get away with it. I rolled with the kick, but it still hurt. And so did the next couple. Otilio made kind of a nervous giggle and kicked me again.

That makes Five, you big, ugly sunuvabitch, I said to myself, *and I'm keeping count.*

"That's enough," Milianos said. "Leave us." Then, in English, "I want to talk to this one alone."

Otilio smiled and started out, but Milianos stopped him: "Not back there. Leave the other one alone for a time."

Otilio muttered something, but he did like he was told, and I figured it was safe to sit up—if I could.

There was something in the cell to sit on: either a big stool or a small bench or an awful idea for a bed, and it was in the shape you expect Mexican jail furniture to be in. Milianos sat on it while I struggled up to sit on the floor—making it look tough, which it was, kind of, but not as bad as I was letting on—and leaned my back against a wall.

"Forgive my impatience," he said politely, "And my lack of manners. My name is Milianos."

"Just call me Culley," I groaned, making out I was hurt pretty bad, "And I don't know why you're upset with that fellow in the next room but-"

"Your friend has told me all about the Gold," Milianos interrupted softly, "He told me how much there is, where it is hidden, and how to get it. Now you will tell me, and when your answers don't agree, I'm going to drop you both down a hole to fiery Hell. And I will drop you slowly. You comprehend?"

"He's not my friend," I grunted, "Just some guy I happened to hook up with. And I don't speak Spanish, but what he was screaming in there sure didn't sound like directions."

"You're smarter than you look." He pulled a cigar, short black, and crooked from his pocket. "I'm glad."

"And I'm sorry you're not as smart as you look." I kept my voice reasonable to make the insult easy to swallow. "Or maybe you've already figured out there's only one way to play this."

"I have my ideas." He put the cigar in his mouth, struck a match on his thumbnail, and stoked it up. It smelled like old burning sweat-socks—which, inside that cell, wasn't bad at all. "But why don't you tell me yours? Please?"

"Think about it," I struggled to sit up a little straighter, and it hurt some. I winced like it hurt a lot before I went on, "And right away it's clear to you we didn't leave that Gold back where we did and cross the desert because we enjoyed the walk. We must've had some damn good reason for it."

"Logical," he blew a cloud of stinking smoke. "A man does not walk away from Gold unless ... Someone was chasing you?"

"Damn close," I said. "Do you know the Serrano brothers?"

"I know of them, I think," he said, "One is a big man, with only one eye?"

"That's them. They had us pinned down. Us and the man who owns the Gold—or used to own it; they killed him. We stashed the Gold and took off across the desert. Now Paco Serrano's sitting on the Gold, only he doesn't know it. Yet."

"And where is this?"

"A few hours by car, but I don't recommend going that way; he can see you coming on the road a good hour before you get there. It's maybe a day's easy ride back across the desert on horseback."

"I don't wish to ask this next question twice," Milianos took a deep drag on that ugly cigar, till the end glowed angry red, and he spoke softly. "Where is it?"

"We'll show you. Both of us."

He shook his head. Smiled, "I think not."

"Then think this: You ain't got much time. Maybe you're too late already. Paco Serrano ain't much for brains, but he's going to figure out what he's sitting on eventually. And he'll find it. Then it's too late for you, and for me too: He'll be rich and we won't."

He studied the end of the cigar. "I could persuade you to tell me, I think."

"You don't look to be the kind of man that takes up with torture."

"Possibly not," he nodded at the compliment. "But for that I have Otilio. Otilio is not a cruel man, not a hard man at all, but somehow, he seems to take pleasure in beating you. Much pleasure. It is odd. I must ask him about this some time. Or perhaps he might tell you, eh?"

"If you mean that overgrown village idiot with the heavy boots, he ain't got the brains." Time to put some effort into selling Milianos on the idea of keeping Ray and me alive. "That tub of guts wouldn't know Truth if Christ hisself slapped him in the face with a handful of it. Now think of this," and I tried not to sound like I was making it up as I went along:

"You pick some friends of yours here. As many as you want. You line up some horses, then—" I paused and made like I was hurting too bad to talk while I waited for the rest of it to come to me. As soon as it did, I said, "—you hand us back our side-arms and we lead you to the Gold."

He smiled.

And I knew I had him then, because the sheer bravado of arming me and Ray again called out to a man like him, same as a pretty gal on a soft bed.

If I judged him right, Milianos wasn't the kind of man who made his way kicking the helpless. But a man who handled himself the way he did couldn't resist the notion of a good fight, with Gold at the end of it—at least not with two men he'd already shaded and done it pretty easy.

"Give you back your guns, eh?"

"There are all kinds of ways to play this," I pushed it. "But that's the smartest. When Ray and I have guns, maybe we don't think you'll just murder us out on the trail. And you'll have all the men you want riding with you, so you know we won't try anything low-down—not real low-down, anyway."

"And when we get to the Gold?"

"If the Serrano boys are still there, we push them off. And when that happens, you'll probably be glad to have two more armed men on your side."

"Especially men I don't like," he mused. "How many ride with the Serranos?"

"The three brothers, of course: Paco, Tony, and one-eyed 'Cento. Tony's wounded, but I'm not sure how bad.

Maybe he can still shoot, maybe not. But if he can, you want to face him with plenty of guns on your side. And 'Cento's still big and mean as ever. Last time I saw, they had four men with them, but I know they went back for more. Let's say they might have as much as a dozen but maybe as few as six."

"Call it ten, then." Milianos dragged thoughtfully on his crooked cigar, then rolled it back and forth between his thumb and forefinger, watching the twisted end flip this way and that, mentally counting the men in town he could take along on an operation like this. "What makes you think they're still there—where the Gold is?"

"Because I told them to wait there for me."

Milianos nodded. "And why are you so certain they have not found it?"

"Because I hid it."

"And what will happen when we kill them and get the Gold?"

"Depends on who's still alive. Ray—that guy over in the next room there—he wants to deliver the Gold to where it's supposed to go. So if he's alive, that's what'll happen, most like. But if it's just you and me," I gave him my best boyish grin and tried not to gag on it, "We can flip a coin or something and decide how to split it up. But I ain't sentimental; if the only ones left are me and the Serranos I'll cut a deal with them."

He liked that. "Tell me this then: is there some good reason I should not take your friend out and shoot him in the Square now?"

"He ain't my friend," I lied. "He's my stand-by. Yours, too. While he's alive and riding with us, I got someone watching my back. And if something happens to him or me, you've still got the other one to show you where the Gold's at."

"It still seems one too many. Give me another reason."

"I'll give you two—One: I ain't going without him, and Two: I ain't going without him."

That riled him some, but I kept on talking, "Yeah, you could beat me till I changed my mind, but you ain't got that kind of time, and you'd rather follow two willing men across the desert than the one you have to keep pushing on the point of a gun."

He took another deep, thoughtful drag on that ugly little cigar and gave me a look like *this sounds like it might be fun and profitable, but way too much trouble.*

"And there's one more thing me and Ray can give you." I all of a sudden remembered Ryckman's deal to sell the Gold in Guanajuato. "One more service we can do: Once you get the Gold—if you do—what have you got? You've got half a ton of Gold, but think on it a minute; what good does it do you? Where can you sell it? Who can you sell it to? You know anyone with that kind of money sitting around?"

He looked thoughtful again and I pushed the point hard. "We do; we got a buyer set up. Think about that: we got a deal with a man who can spin that Gold into money—do you?"

All of a sudden, I saw I'd made a bad mistake just now, when I told Milianos how Ray and me had a buyer lined up, and how we could get all those Gold bars turned into actual money. I'd said it just like that: *We* had a buyer, and *we* could do this.

If Milianos was listening careful, he'd maybe figure out Ray and me was closer together in this partnership than I'd been making out.

But he just stood up and stretched. Puffed on his little stink-weed. Then he looked sleepily down at me.

"I'm going outside where the light is better," he said. "And flip a coin. Do you want Heads or Tails?"

"Heads."

"*Bueno.*" He took a last drag on his cigar. Maybe I looked at it a little hungry. I hadn't had the sinful pleasure of tobacco for almost a year. Anyway, he made as if to hand me the butt, changed his mind, and tossed it in the slop jar.

Then he reached into his shirt pocket, pulled out a fresh one, and handed it to me. Flicked a match with his thumbnail and torched it up while I inhaled. Long and deep. I almost said *muchas gracias* but I caught myself in time.

"Thanks," I said, "That's very thoughtful of you."

"It is Tradition."

And he left me to ponder the meaning of that.

CHAPTER 16

I better explain something now before you get the wrong idea about me and my plans for that Gold.

I told Milianos we should pretty much count Ray out of the deal when the time came, and I'll admit I was half inclined that way myself. Not that I planned on killing Ray, mind you. We'd walked across the desert together, which brings a man close, and I liked talking about women and God with him, and when you come right down to it, I didn't want to be the one to keep him from getting into Heaven if getting there was that important to him.

But I remembered how the sight of that Gold turned me all funny, and I knew without too much figuring that if I was still standing when the dust cleared—nossir, I just wasn't to be trusted to hand over any easy wealth, and so far, there was nothing easy about this job of work.

It bothered me for a little bit till I remembered that the chances of either one of us having that option were too damn narrow to worry over. One or the other of us—or both, most likely—was just bound to wind up dead in a thing like this. So, I just sat back and waited to see if Milianos would kill us right there and then.

Instead, an hour or so after our talk, Milianos moved Ray and me to a back room at the Palacio, where we got a chance to eat, clean up and sleep on something that wasn't the ground—I wouldn't call it a bed, though. Otilio sat outside the door with a shotgun, looking ugly, which he was pretty good at, and cursing at us in Spanish every time old Ernesto—that's the awful cook and bartender from last night—brought us plates of something-or-other to eat.

Seemed like Milianos wanted to get the stink of that jail off us because Ernesto also brought us in a couple buckets of water and something you could call soap if you had a good imagination or a sense of humor. Back in the cell, sometime while Otilio was kicking me around the floor, I must've rolled in something. Whatever it was, it stunk like the Devil's own satanic farts and wouldn't wash out, so Milianos sent in one of his old shirts. Fit me pretty good, and after we'd scrubbed up and while we were getting something in our bellies—I wouldn't call it food, exactly—we both started feeling a little less like stomped tumbleweed and more like human folks.

Then I asked Ray to tell me about this murder he done.

"I'm ashamed to speak of it." He looked at the floor and clutched his tin plate while he talked. "But you have a right to know."

Seems like that ambulance -- the one that's sitting full of Gold waiting for us back at Old Pesos—it belongs to

Ray's daddy. This is years back. They leave that farm they was working on, where Ray got his face cut, and make a good living with that truck, up and down Texas from the panhandle to the Rio Grande, one way and another. But Ray's getting to be older by then, and restless kind of, so he ups and joins the U.S. Army, and after a time gets a soft job as a combat instructor. There's lots of men out west who want to fight an Indian—or a Mexican—and Ray gets paid for teaching them the art of it. Some of them even teach him a thing or two, and life on an Army Base ain't bad if you don't know any better.

Then he gets word his daddy came down sick and wants to go home to die.

Home's here in 'Nada. So Ray leaves the Army to be with him, and drives his daddy's truck for a living down here in Mexico while the old man gets around to dying, which he does in a month or six weeks maybe.

It's after his funeral when the trouble starts.

Ray's sitting out there, in this same cantina, thinking of what he should do with his life now, and old Ernesto's granddaughter, she's called Ciera, comes and sits with him. Ray figures she feels sorry for him., because they ain't talked much before this. She's impressed he can read, and asks him to tell her about his books, which he's got one in his pocket. So, he takes it out and reads her a little from a book called OTHELLO.

It touches her, Ray's reading does. Moves her to tears, the part where Othello says how Desdemona pitied him for his suffering, and he loved her for her pity. Ciera puts her hand on his and they sit like that for a time, listening to the music play on the old gramophone.

Ciera's keeping company in those days with Otilio—our jailer out there. Otilio's away—looking at horses with Milianos, I think—but his younger brother Jorge, he's maybe eighteen or so, and he's sitting in the cantina watching from another table, making a big show of protecting his brother's girl. And he's getting drunk.

He starts talking in a loud voice. Nasty talk. Ciera gets upset and wants to leave, but Ray stops her.

He raised his eyes and looked straight into mine. "I shouldn't have done that. She was Otilio's woman. I had no right." He took a mouthful of food before he went on, and I should mention that old Ernesto's cooking hadn't got any better since last night, so Ray must have been pretty wrought-up telling all this to actually eat the stuff. I remembered the catchy tune about the Crying Woman and wondered if they played that last year when Ray was here. Tried to picture it while he talked:

Jorge comes up to the table, and he's a big shot now, saving his brother's girl from this ugly *gringo*. Ray thinks it over, and to avoid a fight he tells Ciera she should go. But that ain't enough for Jorge. Now he won't let Ciera leave. He leans over the table, right up to Ray's face, and insults him some way. (Ray raised a hand to the side of his face where the scar was and rubbed it without thinking.) So, Ray gets up and hits him.

Later on, he feels pretty bad about how he struck the first blow, like he had no business fighting Jorge. But at the time he's telling about, he can't help it, can't think much at all, and he just gets up and hits the kid.

Even sober Jorge wouldn't be no fight for Ray. Maybe he ain't as drunk as Ray thinks, but he's still no fight for him. Ray makes him look foolish in front of Ciera and everyone else looking on. Ray just hits him wherever he wants, whenever he wants, cuts him down with his hands. So Jorge shoots him.

The way Ray tells it, What else could he do? Young Jorge, he's got no choice if he wants to save face, and the drink's got his blood up, so when Ray throws him against the wall, Jorge pulls his gun and shoots him in the left hand.

He raised the hand for me to see a faint scar. "It was a little thing. A scratch. I should have backed away, but my blood also was up. I took the gun away from the boy and killed him.

"Do you understand? He was unarmed when I killed him—I had his gun. But I didn't think of that. I just took the gun away from him and shot him. In the heart."

"I don't blame you none," I said.

"I blame myself. And I knew others would blame me. I'm an outsider here. An *Americano*. A *gringo*. Milianos and Otilio were away, not in town that night, so escape was easy. I got in my father's truck and drove north.

"Since then I've been in the States, making some kind of living. Trying to decide what to do next with my life. And trying to think of some way perhaps to come back here to my father's home and atone for what happened. Apologize to Ciera. And Otilio, too." He gave me a funny look. "Can you understand how I felt when you opened that map and I saw the only place for us to go was back here to 'Nada? My destiny had caught up with me then," he half-grinned. "I guess it took a roundabout way to do it, but here I must face it and try to pay for my crime."

Well what can you say to that?

I tried to tell him nobody could hardly blame him for doing what he done. Early on in this book I said about how getting shot will just naturally upset a man some, and let me tell you those are still words to live by, but Ray couldn't see it. Maybe he was carrying a load of regret and couldn't get out from under it. I've seen that happen to a man, don't know for sure even now if that was Ray's case. But it sure preyed on his mind some.

When I could see he wasn't going to feel any better talking about Jorge, I got Ray to talking some about 'Nada. And Milianos.

"How'd a man like him get stuck in a one-whore town like this anyway?"

"He was born here," Ray said simply, "He was away fighting in the revolution for a time, of course, and there's the usual story about him and some officer's wife, but he came back and seemed content to stay. 'Nada wasn't always such a forlorn little hole in the desert, you know."

"It wasn't?" I tried another mouthful of whatever it was Ernesto had cooked up for us. It tasted like some old Indian had died cursing the white man's bones and Ernesto had fried him up and melted cheese on it. I took another bite while Ray talked.

"Quenada was quite prosperous once. But when the Government built the new highway south from Saltillo, they built it on the other side of that desert we crossed. And with no big highway, there just wasn't any reason to come here anymore. That's when they started calling it 'Nada. And men began moving out, looking for something better."

"And I guess that 'something better' is us right now: you and me," I nodded toward the door. On the other side, we heard the sounds of low, excited talk. Been hearing it ever since we got there.

"No," Ray said, "It's you and me—and the Gold."

CHAPTER 17

Funny thing is, it seemed to me like most folks drinking and talking out there in the *cantina*, they looked on Ray with a fair amount of favor just now. From what we could hear through the door, they didn't sound a bit sorry to see their old buddy Ray-the-truck-driver back in town again. Not such a bad sort, to hear them tell it. And as for little Jorge, well too bad about him, but you know how these things get out of hand...

I wondered about this at first, but then it hit me that where Ray used to be an outsider, he was now the local boy who came back home and dropped a Gold brick in the middle of Main Street. A thing like that makes folks sit up and take notice, and most of them thought it was a pretty good idea. All night there was this simmering buzz out there: "*El Tapado*"— Mexican for buried treasure, and everyone going on about how much Gold there was, what all it would buy, and how big and important and well-fed the citizens of 'Nada were going to be from now on.

It occurred to me that all this public sentiment was going to make it damned hard to separate the Dutchman's Gold from these folks when the time came, but then I figured that issue would probably come up for election in due course, and no sense counting up votes till we saw how many made it to the polls, so I got some sleep.

And the next morning we left: Me, Ray, Milianos, and eleven men from 'Nada.

Milianos walked us out from the cantina down the street to where Otilio was getting some horses ready. Turned out Otilio owned the local horse livery and gas station, besides being Milianos' deputy. I noticed he treated the horses a damnsight better than he'd treated me, checking their legs and hoofs, seeing them saddled right, and if they looked skittish, he gentled them down by breathing in their nose and talking baby talk. Funny to see that ill-tempered bastard take on like that.

It wasn't long before there were horses, supplies, and Milianos' posse all ready to go. Before we left, he made everyone raise their right hand and swear to follow orders. Then he gave me and Ray our guns and my two boxes of extra rounds. Milianos just handed Ray his Army .45, but he looked thoughtfully at my Harrington first, and then walked up to where I was standing next to some horses.

"*Senor* Culley," he held up my Harrington by the barrel, "You see I give you back your gun, I give you the loan of this fine horse-" He patted the side of a fat brown Arabian gelding. "-I even give you the shirt off my back that you wear."

"And I'm all overcome with gratitude about it," I said.

"I have gone to some trouble for you." He still had that thoughtful look, "I feel responsible. Tomorrow I hope you and I may find some arrangement—how do you say? —to our mutual benefit. Take care. It would sadden me to see you killed. Truly."

"It would sadden me to get killed," I said. "Truly. Deeply too, while we're at it. Now you want to hand me that iron?"

He smiled his best lazy white-tooth smile.

"For my part." He handed me the gun. "To be shot with a tiny thing like this would be insulting."

More bad-mouth about my .22. We'd see when the time came. Meanwhile, I said I'd try to keep the party polite, strapped the Harrington on my hip, stowed the extra rounds in my pockets, and went to get the animal they had for me.

Just then, as I was walking behind him, Otilio—he was sitting up in the saddle on the second-best horse in the bunch—Otilio backed up his horse and it kicked me. Didn't hurt much. A mistake maybe.

Otilio snickered.

Now I hate to do harm to a dumb animal, but in this case, I made an exception. I grabbed Otilio's saddle and jerked it sideways, and when he spilled off, I used the toe of my boot to roll him right under his horse's legs. Then I grabbed the reins in one hand and my hat in the other and spooked the poor critter back and forth while the big man underneath tried to roll clear, screaming with the pain and scare of it.

You know, it kind of surprised me how much I enjoyed that.

Yeah, I owed the big sunuvabitch a few kicks, maybe. But it still surprised me how much I liked hearing him scream, the sound of horse hoofs hitting his fat flesh, and the satisfying "squish" when the animal put his weight on squirming Otilio.

Better watch that, I told myself.

Someone pulled me away and someone else helped Otilio out from under, got him up on his feet, then held him back while he made like he wanted to come at me, and we traded the usual dirty looks and insults, but I got the best of this because I was still pretending I didn't speak Spanish.

Then there was nothing to do but ride out. Milianos was sure making a big production out of this, and I wondered about that a little till I remembered 'Nada was a small town, and where there's small towns, there's talk. Lots of talk.

So it just made sense. If Milianos had killed Ray and me, then rode out and got rich, there'd be talk about it. Likewise, if everyone saw me and Ray leave town at gunpoint and never come back, there'd be talk about that, too.

But if the whole town watched him give us back our guns, swear in a legal posse and all, it'd look a lot better for Milianos to come back rich—no matter what happened to me and Ray.

It was worth thinking about.

I got up on the horse they'd picked out for me, and everyone else got mounted up ... then something happened that hit me all over strange:

Just as we were lining up to head out, with everybody in town standing around to watch and wish us get-rich-quick, then all of a sudden, some young girl—she was sixteen maybe, dark-haired, bright-eyed, and quick as a kitten—all of a sudden, she runs through the crowd, up to Milianos' horse, plants a foot in the stirrup and jumps into his saddle and throws her arms around his neck.

He said something to her I couldn't make out, but my horse started ambling their way in time enough for me to see him pull a button off his shirt and hand it to her, and he says in Mexican, "You will sew this on for me when I return. Keep it until then," and she jumps from his saddle and runs back into the crowd happy as a kid at Christmas.

Like I say, the sight of it, the funny-familiar look of the whole business hit me real peculiar, and Milianos noticed how I was looking. He flicked his reins to set his horse prancing up to mine.

"You are bothered by something?" he asked.

"What I just seen," I said, realizing all-to-once why it looked so spooky-familiar, "I read something in a book once just like it."

"You have read a book once?"

"Yeah." That set-to with Otilio had got me warm. I pulled at my hat brim to get the sweat off my forehead. "There's a part in this book where the hero's going out to rescue a treasure, and before he leaves, some girl jumps up in his saddle, and he cuts the buttons off his vest and gives them to her. Just like you just done."

"Eh?" he gave me a lop-sided grin, "And does the hero get the treasure?"

"Yeah, but he don't enjoy it much."

Later, back at Old Pesos, I got to thinking more about this and I looked through my bookshelves and found the book I was thinking on. It was NOSTROMO by Joseph Conrad, and I got to reading and found out I remembered that part all wrong, but right now it just made me feel funny, kind of.

Not Milianos, though. "Too bad." He flicked a glance at the girl standing in the back of the crowd, clutching that button in her fist. "A man should know how to enjoy a good thing."

And he wheeled his horse and headed us out of 'Nada.

CHAPTER 18

I should tell you something about crossing the desert. It's a lot better riding than walking.

But that ain't saying much.

Back in the States, the horse had been pretty well forgot about as transportation for twenty years and more, but in Mexico, they still seemed to like them. My dad rode horses a lot when he was young, because there wasn't anything else to ride, and every day of his adult life he thanked God and Henry Ford for giving man the automobile.

Myself, I rode the smelly beasts just enough to learn the truth of what they say about a horse being dangerous at both ends and uncomfortable in the middle. And back in the War, I saw mounted Polish Cavalry charge across an open plain and into barbed wire while Germans in trenches opened up machine guns at them—which taught me that when a man gets on a horse, most of the brains in that outfit is behind the saddle.

So I wasn't kindly disposed to horses in the first place, and the one they give me didn't win my heart. He was a fat brown Arabian gelding with arthritis and a mind of his own. Not the kind to run out from under you, but he might take a notion to wander off on some personal errand unless you kept pulling his head where you wanted it to go. And he was so fat the strap that went around his belly and held the saddle on (The cinch, they call it.) that strap kept working loose, and the saddle would slip and I'd have to stop and tighten it.

Ray rode a rangy black Mustang that could probably tell some interesting stories about his wild youth, but he was a long time dead now, or looked it, and Ray had to keep him moving by main force. He was a good rider, though—better than me, anyhow—and managed him pretty good.

Couple of things I noticed about those horses: When Milianos picked them, he chose two that would get us where we were going, but wouldn't be any trouble to chase down if it came down to a chase. Also, he hadn't brought any pack animals along.

He hadn't brought any pack animals along. Well maybe he figured they could fix Ray's ambulance and just drive out with the Gold.

Or maybe he figured when he left Old Pesos Mine there'd be plenty of empty horses to carry the load.

Not that we'd told him we were going to Old Pesos. Not right off, anyway. But he wasn't dumb, and when I said it was a day's easy ride, he probably narrowed it down—there just ain't that many places to go to in a desert. And when I mapped out a route to a water hole about halfway there, he was probably nine-tenths sure.

The water hole we headed for wasn't the one Ray and I had stopped at. We were riding across the desert and making better time, so we could run a straighter line than Ray and I had been able to do afoot. I figured to noon at that water hole, but it was closer to two by the time we got there, thanks mainly to Ray's horse and my riding.

Oh yeah, I want to tell about that: Somehow Otilio seemed to figure it was his job to criticize my riding. If I yanked hard on the reins, he was right there to scream curses at me for hurting an animal. "*Hijo de la flauta*" seemed to be his favorite name for me, which would have hurt my feelings some if I minded being called a Son of a Flute. I'd been in Mexico long enough to know that's a pretty serious thing to call a man down there, but it never bothered me much—leastways not as much as the tone of voice Otilio always put it in.

So if I rode the animal, I was doing it wrong by his book, and if I stopped to tighten the cinch, it was either too tight or too loose, but he couldn't be bothered to get down and do it for me. He just sat up there on his horse and screamed instructions at me—in Mexican, which I was pretending not to understand, remember. I noticed, though, that he yelled some at everybody else. so maybe he just liked horses. Sure preferred them to my company, anyhow.

One last thing: On American saddles, there's a leather handle they call a saddle horn. It's right out in front where it's easy to hold on to if you want to sit a little steadier, but if you use it, cowboys look at you like you just cheated at cards. On Mexican saddles that part is about as big as a writing desk, and the back of the saddle comes up just like a rocking chair or something, so it's just natural to take hold of that saddle horn. Which got me yelled at even more by Otilio, and snickered at by the experienced *vaqueros*.

Guess that's something else I don't understand about horses and Mexicans. And something to occupy my mind while I tried to stay on top of that monster.

Like I say, we got to the water hole maybe two in the afternoon, and it was a pretty good water hole, with big rocks for shade, and plenty of scrub-trees around. As soon as we got there, everyone dismounted and looked after their horses. I started to, but Otilio jerked the reins out of my hand and did it right, calling me a stupid *gringo* son-of-a-flute.

Milianos came up to Otilio about that time, leading his horse easy as you wear a wrist-watch. He looked at me, then at Otilio, and smiled.

"Don't be so hard on the *Americano*," he said in Mexican, "He's not such a bad sort."

Otilio spat. "He's a stinking gringo, and tomorrow when he shows us the Gold, I will kill him."

"Why so angry with this one?" Milianos glanced my way to make sure I wasn't understanding any of this. "It was not he who killed Jorge."

Now when someone is talking about you and you're pretending not to know it, you want to act ignorant, but not too stupid. Otilio's tone of voice didn't leave much doubt about who he was talking about or his general opinion on the subject. So instead of giving Milianos my usual idiot grin, I tried to look puzzled and upset while Otilio talked.

"...a fair fight," he was saying, "I am his brother and he was mine, but it was a fair fight. I cannot be too mad at the one who killed him, though I will kill that one also when the time comes. But this one, he brings to mind another such—" He got himself under control, calmed down all over sudden and spoke almost reasonably to the big lawman while he tended the horses:

"My father worked for a time on a ranch in Texas. Jorge and I lived with him in the bunkhouse. Jorge was just a tiny one then. Our mother died giving birth to our baby sister, God rest them both. I watched over little Jorge and saw that he was no trouble. I was a good hand with the horses even then, and sometimes they gave me a few pennies when I helped to brush them out or clean the hoofs, and I was proud when I gave that money to my father, for we were poor."

Well, he'd be right about that, anyway. Cowboys' wages never amounted to much: barely enough for a cowboy to live on, let alone a cowboy and two kids. Otilio took the saddle and blanket clear off the fat Arabian I'd been riding and started combing him while he talked. "One night the *gringo* who owned this ranch came into the bunkhouse and beat my father. There was no reason. My father had done nothing. But there, in front of the others, and in front of us, his sons, this man beat my father until he cried. My father cried in front of us, his sons.

"We should have left then." He brushed the horse a little harder, then started massaging his hind-quarters, "But there was no money. My father had to work the rest of the week until pay day. Disgraced. Looked down upon by the others. And at week's end, he was given only half his pay and ordered to leave.

"We could not leave with so little. My father had to beg for more, in front of us, his sons." Otilio looked at me and his voice got hard again. "He begged. And the *gringo* just laughed."

He moved from the horse's hind-quarters to his shoulders and rubbed some more like he was trying to work the anger out of himself. And not doing a real good job of it. "This one is like that other. The same look of self-pride and stupidity. And I will kill this one. Slowly. I will shoot his knees off and make him crawl. When he begs for water, I will cut off his *cojones* and stuff them down his throat one at a time and laugh as he chokes them down. Then, much later, when he begs for death..." he looked my way and grinned. "...I believe I will pluck out his eyes, fill his mouth with salt, and set him to wander in the desert."

Milianos just stood there in front of him, getting all this, and his face never changed once. When Otilio finally wound down, Milianos said in a tone I couldn't quite figure: "That is good, Otilio. Then, years from now, you can look back on what you did to this Americano and have pride. A man should have something like that. A thing to remember and be proud of." He pulled a short black cigar from his shirt pocket, thought for a moment, then put it back.

"But remember this first," he said finally. "You do nothing to either of them until we have the Gold. Then you do what you wish. But not until then. It is understood? You hurt not the one nor the other while we need them. I would hate to die poor because of you, Otilio. And you would hate that too. It is understood?"

"I have your promise on this?"

"I have yours?"

"As I am a man of honor," Otilio said solemnly, "I don't hurt them until we have the Gold. Then I kill that one quick and this one slowly. And painfully. And I have your word?"

"My promise," Milianos said, "As I am a man of honor."

I couldn't figure quite how he meant that, whether he was really going to let Otilio cut me to little pieces or if he was just stringing him on. But he was sure enough stringing one of us, and I didn't like the odds it wasn't me.

About time I played dumb some more. I went up to them, looked at Otilio, and said to Milianos,

"*Senor* Milianos, I can't make out what this fat tub said about me, but tell him the same goes for him and all his family back to the dog that whelped his great-grandmother." Milianos smiled. I kept talking, "Now I'm going to get in a little target practice. You just make sure he doesn't mess his pants at the sound of gunfire."

Milianos told Otilio that he had scared me so much I had to go shoot my gun just to get my courage back up. As I left, I recalculated those odds again, and decided whatever way I played the game, I Milianos was no safe bet.

So I better do something about those odds.

CHAPTER 19

I walked out a ways to a likely-looking scrub-tree. Ray started to join me, but I made a quick sign, "no," and he picked right up on it. If Milianos saw us talking now, he might guess I knew what he and the horse-lover was saying about us.

I'd packed two boxes of .22-shot across the desert in my pockets, and Milianos gave them both back to me before we started out, so I had about a hundred rounds on me, plus the nine rounds there in the Harrington. Seemed to me that no matter what kind of shooting scrape we got into, nobody was going to let me re-load ten times, and I could probably put that ammunition to better use before we got to Old Pesos.

I'd picked up an old newspaper at the Palacio in 'Nada, and right now I walked up to the scrub-tree and hung a sheet of it about the size of a man's chest on the thorns. Then I stepped off thirty long paces and commenced to shooting.

Shooting is a thing that takes steady practice—for me it does, anyhow. Back in the War, I started carrying my side-arm in a big leather holster with a flap over it, which is good for keeping out mud, sand, and scorpions, but it slows a man up some getting it out, so I got the habit of wearing it butt-forward on my left side so I could lift the holster flap with my left hand and pull out the Harrington with a fancy right-hand cross-draw, which used to impress a lot of folks back in Kansas City, times when they needed impressing.

But I didn't try none of that now. Not in front of these boys. I just drew slowly and aimed my first shot at the upper left corner of the paper, just to make sure the Harrington still shot straight.

It did.

It felt good in my hand, the familiar grip, the easy ham-mer, and the heavy seven-inch barrel that never kicked up on me. I picked out a twig just above the paper and spent five shots whittling it back. Missed it twice. There were three shots left in the cylinder when I stopped and re-loaded.

The Harrington is a single-action piece, which means you have to thumb the hammer back before you pull the trigger. Slows me up some, but I'm not that fast to start with. I shoot two-handed by preference—left hand steadies the gun and cocks the hammer, right hand shoots—but I long ago learned the trick of thumbing back the hammer right-handed while I aim, so I can shoot with one hand if I have to.

I'm a thoughtful shot. Learned that about myself when I was working for Seamus Feeney back in Kansas City.

There's some men can pull and shoot a gun quick as you sneeze, but I got to have a half-split-second to line up the sights, and another half-split-second to ponder the ethics of the situation, and that whole split-second, that's just long enough to put me right out of the competition when it comes to serious shooting.

Oh, I did all right in the War, and I could hold my own against most of the Kansas City punks, but that was just amateur stuff. Up against someone like Tony Serrano—probably Milianos too—I was a safe bet to place second, and they don't give prizes for second place in a gunfight.

So I figured maybe I better try something cute. After I re-loaded, I put a hole in the paper close to the bottom and just off-center. Then I picked another twig and spent five rounds trimming it back. Missed once. Then I re-loaded.

A few men watched me from the shade, but no one felt like getting out in the sun and coming over. Mostly they just sat there and made comments on how seldom I hit the paper.

Just what I wanted.

The cylinder in the Harrington carried nine rounds, but I only shot six at a time, then stopped and re-loaded, hoping maybe someone was keeping count. And I put most of my shots on the tree, not on the paper.

Fifty rounds later, I had trimmed eight twigs close back to the branches, so I knew I could hit a spot the size of a man's thumb five times out of six at thirty paces. But I only had seventeen shots showing on the paper, scattered wide across it.

Nice shooting, Culley.

Milianos came up beside me and looked at the paper.

"*Puedo?*" he asked.

I gave him a blank look.

"May I?" He pointed at the paper and tapped the pistol in his right holster.

"All right," I said, "But try not to get any holes in it, I haven't finished the crossword puzzle."

I turned to look, and that was all the time it took him to pull the gun off his right hip and put three shots square in the middle of the paper, almost touching each other. He holstered it, and at the same time pulled his left gun and squeezed off three rounds that tore the paper clean off the tree and sent it soaring in the wind. All of a sudden, his right was out again, and a round caught the paper on the fly. He fired his left, missed, then hit the swirling paper with a second shot that blew it to ribbons.

Back in the shade, everyone cheered his shooting. Milianos just smiled at me while he jerked the clips from his guns and reloaded.

I walked back to my horse, listening to the comments on my shooting and pretending not to understand them, took a bottle of solvent from the saddlebag, and started cleaning the Harrington.

And making my plans.

CHAPTER 20

I haven't told much yet about the men from 'Nada, the men who rode out with us but never rode back. They were a tough-looking crowd. Not hard or mean, maybe, but most of them had worked their time in one revolution or another, and each one knew how to get along with serious trouble.

Now, though, they were farmers and tradesmen: men like me and Ray, I guess, who could handle a fight, still, but didn't do it on a regular basis. The only one in the posse who made a steady living off his guns was Milianos the law-man, and we were going up against sure-enough *banditos*.

I sure hoped we had them outnumbered real good.

The only ones I knew close-up were Milianos, Otilio, and old Ernesto, the chess-playing bartender and god-awful cook back at the Palacio. Ernesto had a rifle slung on his saddle that was the longest single firearm I ever saw in my life—looked to shoot right through a man and kill someone in the next county. Man carries a gun like that, he probably uses it pretty good, and it made me feel better to see we had long-range artillery on our side. Funny how that turned out.

As for the others, there was one guy and all I remember about him was that he had the bloated-up, dead-look face of a man that's drunk a bottle of tequila every night for twenty years. Always seemed to be staring at the horizon and didn't talk much. Then there was a chubby-built little fellow named Diego, who owned a pretty decent farm by 'Nada standards. There was a long-faced man in his sixties who helped out Otilio sometimes, and most of the rest had worked at the factory till it closed down last year. Guess they hadn't moved out right away and now they were just broke, hungry, and looking for something better. Ray said he felt kind of bad about them.

I mentioned back there that these men rode out with us and didn't ride back, so I might as well say it now: All that came out of that desert the next afternoon was me, Ray, and the Dutchman's Gold. And one other, but I'll get to that part later.

Anyhow, after we watered the horses, fed ourselves, and rested some, everybody saddled up for the last leg of the trip. Before we left, Ray and I told Milianos we were headed for Old Pesos.

"We'll be coming in from the West," Ray said, "But then we circle, towards the edge of a cliff where there's a foot path down to the mine itself. No good for horses, but a man can walk it easily. We won't get there much before nightfall anyway, and if we go in at Dawn, we'll have the Sun behind us."

Milianos nodded thoughtful-like, pulled a cigar from his shirt pocket, looked at it, then went ahead and stoked it up.

"Good enough," he said when he had it going, "But why not go in under cover of night?"

"Because that cliff face gets dark at night," I said, "And I don't fancy picking my way down there in the pitch-black."

"Besides," Ray put in, "There's a good place to stop and get organized just about an hour's walk this side of the cliff. You know best, perhaps, but I will fight better if I can get off my horse for a time first. And as I say, then we hit them at dawn."

"We shall see." Milianos took a long drag on his cigar and exhaled a cloud of black smoke that hung twisted in the desert air a second before it lost interest and blew apart. He got on his horse without another word and we rode out.

The next leg of the trip went slow. I've seen dead things move faster than Ray's horse, and by that time, riding mine had turned into a balancing act to keep the saddle from sliding off. So it was easy enough for us to slip back out of earshot and hold a little conversation:

"Don't let this shock your tender sensibilities, Ray," I said casually and in English, "But these men mean to kill us and take the Gold for themselves."

Ray nodded.

"They don't speak so frankly near me," he said, "But from their talk, they have many plans for the Gold—and none say anything about sharing with *Mijnheer* Ryckman's widow."

"Milianos opened up with the big stable-boy back there, and it seems they've pretty much set their hearts on killing you. And Otilio waxed kind of eloquent on the subject of what he's going to do to me if he gets that chance."

Ray looked at the dozen men riding in front of us and he rode on silent for a bit. Then, "I wish there were some way short of all that killing," he sighed, "Some other way to keep the promise."

"Maybe when it comes down to it, we can work something else out," I said, "But I got to say, Milianos and Stable-Boy are going to be hard to talk around to it."

"You're right." Ray nodded sadly, "I don't know... I guess I just hoped .... What I told you about making up for my sin by keeping that promise to *Mijnheer* Ryckman: it seemed to me then like something a man could do with honor."

"Not now?"

"Now it's starting to look complicated." Ray got a look on his face. It wasn't as ugly as his smile but it wasn't a pleasant sight either. I didn't say anything right away. It worried me some to have my partner riding into a shooting scrape with an attitude like that. And he still seemed pretty fixed on the notion of taking all that money back to the Dutchman's woman. Then I remembered:

"Seamus Feeney used to say something," I offered, "We'd get in a situation sometimes that maybe called for us to act real unpleasant, and he'd say 'Set your priorities, gentlemen.'"

"Meaning?"

"I told you I made money running hooch in those days, but the fact is, we were gangsters, us boys that worked for Feeney. Not much different maybe from the Serrano Brothers—some ways maybe not as good." I hung on to that saddle tighter, trying to talk and ride a horse at the same time.

"Seamus had a philosophy. Not much, as philosophy goes, but he was a gangster, like I said, and sometimes in that line of work you have to do something kind of awful. Or maybe talk someone else around to doing it. I look back on things I did for gunman's wages back then, I'm not real proud of it. But times like that, he always told us to step back and decide what's important. 'Set your priorities, gentlemen' he'd say, 'Make up your mind to what matters, then let the rest line up behind—'"

But before I could go on, my saddle slipped clean loose of that fat horse and I had to jump off and tighten the cinch. Which was Otilio's excuse to ride back and scream at me. Again.

I just looked up at him and got a picture in my mind of him lying dead in the desert.

Cheered me considerable.

CHAPTER 21

It was full dark by the time we reached our stopping place, a couple miles from the top of the cliff at Old Pesos. There was a sheltered spot with a rocky outcrop where you could build a fire and it wouldn't be seen. About fifty yards away was an arroyo filled with dry jack-brush and a blasted scrub-tree on the far side—shaped like a crooked cross.

This was far enough from Old Pesos to be safe, but everyone moved as quiet as they could in the dark there, with Otilio taking special care with the horses. There wasn't any water up here, but the animals could smell it down at Old Pesos, and they thirsted for a drink. Otilio made sure to fill the water-bags at our last stop though, and he kept them quiet, letting them drink while he whispered to the restless ones and saw to their comfort. I noticed old Ernesto built his fire Apache-style, just glowing embers with no flame or smoke.

Ernesto warmed up *tortillas* and *frijoles* with some kind of meat that tasted like stomped cat. When we had our fill—which didn't take much—Ray and me went up to Milianos, who was sitting by Ernesto's little fire looking relaxed and comfortable.

"You thought much about how we're going to do this operation tomorrow?" I asked.

"Yes I have." Milianos looked at us seriously. "I think the best thing to do is go in, kill them all, and take the Gold."

"No more plan?" Ray asked politely, "No strategy?"

"Ummmm," Milianos pursed his lips in thought for a second, "No."

We just stood there. When he saw we weren't going away, Milianos finally asked, "Have you two a plan, then?"

"Lookee here," I hunkered down in front of him. "You got any idea what we're walking into?"

I made a rough map in the dirt for his benefit. First a straight line with three breaks in it: "This is the cliff where we'll come down tomorrow, Sunrise," I showed him, "These three spots are where there's tunnels into the cliff. Shouldn't be anyone in them, 'cause they ain't real cozy after dark, but you never know."

Then I drew a line with a curve in it, coming out right-angle from the first line, "This is a packed-earth road that runs from the mine in the cliff down to the bridge and fence at the bottom of the gravel slope. There's a ditch runs along either side of this road, but everything else down that slope is gravel: hard to walk on and damn-near impossible to walk up."

I made a mark on the north side of the road, close to the cliff face. "This is the engine shack," I said, "It's where they used to house the heavy machines, and if Serrano knows we're coming and wants to fort up, this is the place he'll do it —-"

Ernesto piped up from over my shoulder, "You mean big stamping machines?" I turned to see him and a couple other men had gathered around. "A big building? Very tall?" he asked.

I wasn't surprised to see he spoke English. Something about him at the Palacio told me he understood more than he let on.

"No," I explained, "They never did much fine stamping at Old Pesos, and the building they did it in burned down years back. This is just a small building. But heavy-built."

"What is inside, then?" Ernesto asked.

"Nothing now. Used to be they had a heavy steam engine in there, and they run belts or chains or whatever from the engine in that shack to run equipment in the mineshaft."

And they made the walls heavy and the openings small in case the damn thing blew up some day. But no point going into that now, just so Milianos understood what a tough nut it could be.

"It's on the high ground," I went on, "There's a well inside, and there's only one door and no windows, but narrow vents—four to a side, waist-high, about as wide as a man's hand and arm-length apart, where they used to run the belts through—good to shoot out of but tricky to shoot into."

I made a mark next to the engine shack. "Here's a water tower nearby. Tallest spot in the mine, but there's no cover."

Milianos looked bored now, but I kept going, made a mark on the other side of the road. "The office is over here, and there's not much to it, but a couple men could hide there if they kept low."

I moved my finger, made a bigger mark on the south side of the road, closer to the cliff face, almost straight across from the engine shack. "This is the bunk house and kitchen, and it's the most comfortable place in the whole set-up. If there's any number of men there, and they've been there any length, and if we catch them by surprise, that's where they'll be. Let's hope so, 'cause there's plenty of windows, and a door on every side. Easy place to take if we have to."

Still the bored look from Milianos, but a few more of the others came up to look over my shoulder. Old Ernesto leaned over and rubbed his chin, studying. He played chess, I remembered. I made marks to point out a storage shed and the privy, further down the slope and Milianos finally got off his butt for a closer look.

"This you say is the strong point?" He pointed at the engine shack. I nodded. "But this is where we'll most likely find them," He pointed at the bunk house, then traced his finger, "And this is the best path to walk?"

"About the only path to walk, unless you like wading in gravel," I said.

Ray spoke to him in Spanish, "There are ditches on each side of the road, deep enough for temporary cover, and you could flank—"

Milianos interrupted, talking to me in English, "And you don't know where the Serranos will be."

"Like I say, probably the bunk house, but—"

"And you don't know how many men are with them."

"I told you back in 'Nada, maybe six or more; ten maybe—"

"You're not even sure he's there at all."

"If I was betting—"

"Here's the plan, then," He put his fist on the line marking the cliff. "We go in..." Pushed his fist across the map, sluffing it back into the dust "...kill them all and take the Gold."

Everyone cheered. The ones who spoke English translated for the ones who didn't and everybody cheered again.

Except old Ernesto.

And Ray and me.

I was wondering if Milianos was really that bad of a General, or if maybe he didn't want a whole lot of fellow-survivors to share the Gold with.

Found out the next day, though.

Meanwhile, Ray just turned to me in the mostly-dark and said, "I'd like to read a good book right now."

"I know what you mean."

Ray turned back to Milianos. "*Senor* Culley is upset," He said in Spanish, "I should talk to him alone. We're going to walk out to that arroyo," He pointed to the crooked-cross-shaped scrub-tree. "No farther."

Milianos, still enjoying his joke, just nodded.

He 'bout choked, though, when me and Ray came back five minutes later, carrying guns up to our tonsils.

These were the guns we stashed in that arroyo—marked by the lightning-blasted scrub-tree—back when we started out, and we'd never discussed it, but I guess me and Ray always figured to steer Milianos and his posse back to those same whereabouts. So we just naturally meant to sneak back there first chance and load up as much that was deadly as we could tote.

Just natural, yeah, but I left that part out when I explained things to Milianos. And so did Ray. Now we were heavy-armed, it come on everyone as kind of a shock.

Milianos handled it pretty good, though. Old Ernesto pointed to us as we walked slowly back toward camp. Ray carried his Winchester and two Army .45s, I had the Dutchman's Carbine, and we each had a scattergun slung off one shoulder. Plus a couple ammo belts. We probably looked like death come calling, walking the fifty-so yards back from the arroyo. As we came into the dim fire-glow, I saw the men nudge each other and look our way, and I swear I heard a collective fart pass across the assemblage.

But nothing shook Milianos much. He just got up and walked out to meet us halfway. There were maybe three feet between us when he stopped and we did likewise.

"I see you brought us more guns." He took a drag off what was left of his crooked little black cigar. The burning tip lit up his face some, but in the dark there with the faint campfire behind him, it was hard to read his expression.

"That's right," Ray looked him straight-on, "We brought *us* some guns."

Milianos breathed out smoke and his left hand strayed down near his gun-belt. "Give me the rifles," he said evenly, "And the shot-guns. I will pass them among the others."

I just snorted. Ray made his voice very reasonable and said, "You want to back down from this. We're not giving you the guns. You could take them -perhaps- but you don't want to."

Milianos took another drag. He was holding the cigar where he could flick it at one of us while he drew and shot the other. I figured he could get away with it, too, but he just said, "You think not?"

"I know not," Ray said, "We're too close to the mine. Too close to the Serrano brothers—who are still there and you know it. A shot now, they hear it, and maybe build up a fort in the engine shack, as Culley showed you. Or maybe they bring their men through the dark and find us here in the open."

"You are right perhaps," Milianos breathed smoke at us. "But only partly so. Certainly, the Serranos—if they are still there—will hear shooting, and this could cause some inconvenience. But against this possibility, you must weigh the pleasure I will surely get from killing the both of you."

"And finding the Gold without us?" It was about time I said something. "And finding someone to sell it to?"

"Again," he almost shrugged. "Inconveniences."

"Then weigh this," Ray stepped right up in his face, "You took us both down easily enough back in the Palacio after the desert had baked us. But we are rested now," and all of a sudden brought the Winchester right up and stuck it in the lawman's stomach. "And I seldom miss at this range,"

I'd forgot how Ray could move that fast – surprised Milianos some too, from the look of him.

But Milianos didn't say a word. He just raised his left hand from his gun-belt and scratched his head. Then there was a quick blur of motion as the hand came down, batted Ray's Winchester away from his belly, and grabbed the barrel. Hard.

The next step would be to pull the Luger from his right hip and work it some, but Milianos didn't do that. He just stood real still for a second, then let go of the gun barrel, the way you throw a fish back in the water because it's too small.

"Tomorrow," he said, "When we dispose of the *banditos*. I only need one of you to show me to the Gold," he smiled at Ray. "It won't be you."

He turned his back on us and walked to the fire.

CHAPTER 22

I breathed. Seemed like a while since I done it, too. "Dang,
Ray," I managed, "That was kind of a near thing."

"We came close, I think." He nodded and we started
back towards the fire.

"Didn't know you could move like that."

He made that scar-faced grin. "I taught Combat in the
Army, remember. You can do anything if you do it fast
enough."

"I'll keep that in mind," I chewed on it a minute, then,
"How you fancy your chances coming up against that tough
bastard tomorrow? He'll be looking to—"

"He sure will," Ray considered, "I have to take him, I
guess. Maybe we'll get lucky and the Serrano brothers will
do him for us. We'll see. For tonight, though, do you think
we should sleep out in the arroyo?"

"Naah," I said, "It'd just worry the rest of them. By now
Milianos has told them No Shooting, so we're safe enough."

"We'll take turns sleeping."

We settled ourselves up against a good-sized rock a little ways from where everyone else had laid down by the fire. I found out guns weren't the only thing Ray got out of our stash; he pulled a piece of candle and a beat-up book of THE ADVENTURES OF ULYSSES by someone-or-other out of his jacket and we settled down—our backs to the rock, facing the others. Ray turned to me.

"I'm at peace now with what I have to do tomorrow," he said quietly. "I thank you for that."

"How you mean?"

"What you said about setting your priorities. I've been thinking about it. Your friend Seamus Feeney was wise: To decide what's important and let the rest fall into place: '*Set your priorities, gentlemen.*'"

"And you set 'em?"

"I have to keep our promise to *Mjjnheer* Ryckman if I want to get into Heaven. And I certainly don't intend to burn in Hell. Tomorrow, if I have to kill..." he left the rest of that thought for me to pick up on.

"Suppose you die trying?" I asked. "Chances likely, both of us will. You reckon you'll still get into Heaven if you die trying?"

"You know what they say about good intentions, and the road they pave," he said gently. "Now you better sleep some, Culley."

I didn't sleep, of course. Don't know about the men from 'Nada, maybe they slept, but not me. That near set-to with Milianos had shook me up some, and I couldn't help thinking about the next day and the odds against us.

There was me and Ray on one side; the Serrano boys on the other, and Milianos and his posse on the third side, which was a lot of beef to be pushing around. I quit worrying about Ray's attitude—the way he stood up to Milianos settled any question about Ray—but now I worried on my own count.

I said a few pages back that I'm not the high-card when it comes to gun games—slow and steady, that's my style— and from what I knew about how the Serrano brothers handled artillery, and what I'd seen of Milianos' shooting ... well, things was looking dark for our hero, that's all. Every time I closed my eyes, I got a picture of me at the business end of somebody else's gun, or I saw 'Cento Serrano, his one good eye and his big, ugly hands. I even thought about Otilio's plans for making a summer project out of killing me slow, and I figured I really ought to kill him first, then wondered if I'd get the chance... and then the whole question of what to do about Ray and the Gold if I ever got to the end of this—finally I just gave up on it and opened my eyes.

"Sleep well?" Ray asked.

"All right," I yawned, "How's the book?"

"I only got as far as the Cyclops," he set down ADVENTURES OF ULYSSES and stretched his arms "You know, he must have really loved that woman."

"Ulysses? Who'd he ever love?"

"No, Ryckman I mean," Ray said, "There was something in that book about how Ulysses kept trying to get back to his wife— that got me thinking about *Mijnheer* Ryckman again," he reached back behind him as he talked, and snuffed out the last of the candle with his thumb. "How he died, just trying to make his wife proud."

"Must be some kind of woman, that Mrs. Ryckman."

The moon never really come up much that night, and now it was clear down, the only light was kind of a faint red from Ernesto's fire. There was no movement there, just the lumpy shapes of still bodies. I could kind of see them now, silhouetted in the glow.

"*Mijnheer* Ryckman spoke a lot about her as we drove down here." In the dark, there was just Ray's voice, soft and thoughtful-like. "And from the things he told me, I'm surprised she didn't make the trip down with him, share the risk."

It don't surprise me none, I thought.

But I said, "Some women just ain't up to a thing like this. Most women, maybe."

"Maybe so," he yawned big, "But the way he talked about her..." And he fell asleep.

I thought about it some: what kind of woman Ryckman had died for. Funny, thinking about it relaxed me some. Still didn't sleep, but I rested up good.

I been kind of a long time getting around to telling about that shooting scrape at Old Pesos, but I've got a few things to say before I get there. Anybody in a hurry, they can just skip the rest of this next page or so.

First thing: I figured us to be walking into a pretty mean fight, but I didn't know at the time just how ugly it was going to turn out. See, I never knew the Serrano Brothers back when they were sure-enough *banditos*; I only knew them as two-bit bootleggers, and never stopped to think how they used to make a living hiding out and killing when they had to. Didn't know Paco Serrano made it a habit to put out scouts, lay ambushes, and generally make his boys hard to kill. And Milianos didn't know the Serranos at all, so neither one of us was quite ready for what come our way.

Second thing, and this has to do with History: Back in college, a professor lectured to a class full of bright young students and me about how warfare developed from crude barbarity to its present state of advanced civilization. He drew charts and pictures on the blackboard, and he showed how war was such an advanced science now, we'd never have another one.

Well I'm here to say that fight at Old Pesos like to set warfare back a thousand years. Remember, I was in the biggest war in history—up to then, anyway—so I knew a little about the stuff they call carnage and chaos. But I never saw such a mess as the one I got into there.

Final thing: I came out alive (Maybe you guessed that.) but this business of killing folks is bad for a man's character. That fight got me to thinking the best way to solve a problem is to shoot at it; it made me blood-stupid and short-fused, and that attitude got me into a lot of trouble later on in life.

Just thought I'd mention it.

CHAPTER 23

Now though, it was still mostly dark, but the sun was coming up pretty soon when the men from 'Nada roused up and Milianos got this thing organized. Old Ernesto passed out *tortillas*, and everyone tried to eat some but didn't have much luck with it. First one *companero* threw up, and that set off two or three more, and it occurred to me that maybe I wasn't the only one scared in this man's army. Or maybe it was just Ernesto's cooking.

Milianos looked good, though. Damn good. He laughed, slapped a few backs, and went around checking everyone's guns and ammo. Then he turned to Otilio. "You wait here with the horses," he said.

Stable-Boy looked half-relieved at not having to mix it up in the fight, and half-worried someone might take his share of the Gold. Milianos pretended not to notice. "Keep them quiet and hobbled," he went on, "There may be much noise and we don't want to lose horses. When there has been no shooting for perhaps five minutes, you come and help-" he glanced my way for a split-second. "-help me find the Gold." Otilio caught on, brightened considerably, and saw to the horses. For everyone else, though, it was Closing Time at Old Pesos.

And I was scared. Bad scared.

Knew what to do about it, though. What we did back in the war, times like these when you're walking into harm's way and no help for it. I started singing, softly to myself:

"Oh, Danny boy,

The pipes, the pipes are calling..."

Ray heard me. He'd been in the Army too, and probably some old-timer told him how we used to do. And he answered back, singing soft:

"From glen to glen,

And down the mountainside..."

He had a voice like a coyote trapped in quicksand, Ray did, but singing soft helped some. I answered back:

"The summer's gone,

And all the roses falling..."

And he came back with

"'Tis you, 'tis you,

 must go,

And I must bide."

Probably nigh onto twenty years since I sung that song last time, walking alongside a thousand other stupid young men across a blasted field to certain death. *Danny Boy* was the favorite song in the trenches back then. Old Black-Jack Pershing, he didn't like it much. Said he'd rather us sing something we could march to, and that made us like it even more. Cheered me up, it did.

So Ray and me sang together on the chorus, not loud, and sure not pretty, but good enough for this occasion:

"But come ye back,
When Summer's in the Meadow ..."

The men from 'Nada looked at us like we were crazy, and muttered to each other.

"Or when the valley's
Hushed and white with snow ..."

Up front, the sky was turning cold blue just ahead of sunrise.

"It's I'll be he-e-e-er,
In sunshine and in sha-a—dow ..."

And I felt like killing something.

"Danny boy, oh Danny Boy,
I love you so-o-o-o!"

We got to the footpath before the sun could silhouette us on the cliff edge and started picking our way down single-file, moving as quiet as we could in the pre-dawn, me and Ray in front to show the path through the rocks down that cliff face. Once we got to the bottom, everybody stopped, hunkered down, and looked around. In the half-shadowed sunrise we could see the whole layout: the cliff wall behind us, the packed-dirt path curving down the gravel slope, and the buildings on either side of it. But we could only see it from this side, near the cliff.

No sign of life.

Milianos told chubby-faced little Diego to run up ahead and check the engine shack. Diego gulped, but did as he was told, skulking off to the door, out of sight where we were, and skipping back right away to report, 'All Clear,' which was a relief—I'd been deep-down scared about getting shot at from in there, and I felt glad now not to have to worry on it. As Diego got back, the sun came full up over the cliff, flooding the gravel slope, the buildings, and the cliff face, all with hard bright light and the threat of heat.

That left the bunkhouse. I looked around, trying to see into it. If the Serrano Brothers were still here, that's where they'd be. But I couldn't see anything from where we were.

Now if I was Milianos, I'd have put a couple men in the Engine Shack, where they could fire on the bunkhouse from protection while the rest of us went around to one side. But Milianos told everyone to fan out in the ditch alongside the road, with the engine shack at our backs, the road in front of us, and the bunkhouse beyond. Then he turned to me and Ray.

"My man checked the engine shack. Your turn now: the bunkhouse."

The way he said it didn't leave no room to argue. Neither did the ten men with guns in their hands backing him up. Ray and I got up out of the ditch and stood for a second at the edge of the road, facing the bunkhouse.

"You think he'll kill us now—" Ray talked soft and tied down his shotgun so it wouldn't swing if he had to run, "—or wait till we've checked the place out?"

"I don't figure him for a back-shooter," I said, "and besides, he wants us alive—for now."

"Let's get started." He got ready to run across the road. "You want to hit the door, or shall I?"

"I'll get it," I said, "you jump to one side and—"

But just then the bunkhouse door swung open.

Real slow.

And there was Paco Serrano, leaning up against the doorway, looking sad as ever.

His eyes took in the two of us standing in the road, plus a near-dozen heads and twice as many guns looking over the ditch behind us.

And for the first time since I knew him, Paco Serrano grinned.

And he kept right on grinning.

Then he looked straight at me and Ray, and he smiled bigger. Big, wide, and scary as Death, till I thought he'd disappear in that dark doorway and just leave his grin hanging there in air, like that cat in Alice-in-Wonderland.

"Culley," he beamed, "my old friend. You came back! It is good to see you once again."

That's when Hell kicked open the gates at the Old Pesos Mine.

Because when Serrano said it, he spoke in Spanish.

To me.

CHAPTER 24

I swung a look at Milianos, and yeah, he'd heard old Paco talking Mexican to me, all familiar-like, and it took just a split half-second for him to figure out what that meant, and he was bringing the point of his rifle around at me when the ends of three guns all-of-a-sudden stuck out from those tall, narrow vents in the engine shack back of him and started hammering the posse from behind.

Some went down at once, cursing Diego's too-quick scouting; some jumped out of the ditch just as more of Serrano's men opened fire from the bunkhouse, and then everybody flew every-which-way.

But I didn't see much of that, because Ray and me went running for the office shack like Hell wouldn't hold us.

It took maybe three seconds for us to get across that road, like three lifetimes. All of that and more. I moved faster than I ever had in my life, but it felt like crawling through hot tar. My legs wouldn't come up fast enough. Gravel flew up and snapped at my ankles, and—I didn't have time to think this out, it just come to me all at once—I realized Milianos must be trying to shoot our legs out. He was trying to cripple us! There his posse was getting shot to shreds behind him, and all the bastard-sunuvabitch could think of was to cripple us!

Ray hit the office shack door just ahead of me, jumped in, spun around, crouched, and started pumping his Winchester back the way we came, all in half the time it takes to say that. I got inside right after him by jumping over his head, and if Paco Serrano had thought to put a man in there ahead of us, he'd have had to write this because I'd be too dead for the job.

He didn't, though. All that happened was about a dozen shots come through the door—maybe half from Milianos and half from the Serrano boys, some from the bunkhouse, and some through the vents in the engine shack—till I jerked Ray back in and slammed the door.

"Did we make it?" I asked.

"You did," Ray said, "I'm not sure about me. Whose job was it to check the engine shack?"

"Whoever it was, he's real sorry about that," I said, "But no kidding, you all right?"

"Not for certain." Ray sat on the floor and pulled up his left pants-leg. There was a gash in the side of his boot, crossways, a long, ragged torn-up hole between ankle and boot-top. It was starting to turn dark and wet. "It feels like he got some muscle." Ray started to take off his boot, thought better of it. "Is there something I can put on this?"

The Serrano brothers had beat the place up pretty good, or their boys had, but I found a book of Robert Burns' poems and gave it to Ray. He pulled some pages out and wadded them into the gash in his boot while I found some friction tape to tie around it. It took time, because every half-minute we checked out a window to see if it looked like company coming. Finally got it done, though.

"Can you walk on that?"

"I wouldn't care to dance, but walking should be all right—" He tested the leg and made a really ugly face. "—for a while anyway."

"Come look at this."

Outside, Milianos' posse had moved a safe distance down the ditch and was shooting back at the bunkhouse and the engine shack, but Serrano's boys were keeping them pinned down pretty good. The way the vents were in the engine shack, about a hand's-breadth wide and arm-length apart, the *banditos* inside could shoot any direction they wanted and stay pretty safe at it. And if the sun got much higher, which it often does in the daytime, it'd fry the posse's brains out there, if they still had any.

No one seemed too worried about us. I figured most of the men on both sides had got so busy jumping and shooting, they'd lost track of the handsome *Americano* and his trusty side-kick here in the office shack. Hoped so, anyway.

The shooting and cussing went on some. And then something happened I'd seen before, back in the War: Everyone started going stupid.

Someone starts shooting, you shoot back, get hurt maybe, get mad for sure, and all of a sudden you got to get up and *do* something. It ain't safe, and it ain't smart, but you just *got* to—like somebody turned off all your brains and set your body loose.

First, while we watched, old Ernesto slid out of the ditch and crawled low on his belly over toward the water tower next to the engine shack, dragging that god-awful-long gun. I don't know if he could have hit anything any better from up there, but the men from 'Nada crouched there in the ditch, they all cheered him on, and I swear he looked like some weird old insect inching his way across the gravel like that. The Serrano boys saw him too, and there was plenty of fire came his way, but nobody got near him much.

He reached the base of the water tower, and this was the signal for the men from 'Nada to step up their shooting and keep the *banditos* off him or spoil their aim some while he climbed to the top.

It was hurtful to watch. The old man's climbing was worse than his cooking, and lugging that cannon up with him didn't help any. There were ten steps up that ladder to the platform on the water tower, and the men from 'Nada sang out for each step Ernesto made, and Serrano's boys cursed his ancient bones and shot harder. Now and again, splinters flew off the ladder when a bullet struck close, but Ernesto just kept at it, and finally, he was close enough to lay his rifle on the platform and pull himself up.

Only he never did it, because Tony Serrano stepped out of the engine shack, one arm in a sling, raised a handgun, shot him, and stepped back in, calm as you please.

Ernesto jerked, grabbed the ladder, and tried to hold on, but he had nothing to do it with. His hand slipped, grabbed, slipped again, one foot went through the ladder, and he fell backward, hung up—head down, feet up, and dead as can be.

Which got everyone a little more stupid.

Three men from 'Nada jumped out of the ditch and charged the bunkhouse like Santa Anna at the Alamo, only not as lucky. One man fell about halfway there, shot in the back from the engine shack. The other two made the bunkhouse door, one of them kicked it open, then jumped backward six feet through the air because a Winchester cut him in two. The third man actually made it in, we heard some shooting, some banging around, then all of a sudden, he flew face-first out a window, gushing blood like a squeezed sponge.

I got a look at him as he landed, and it surprised me some to see it was the bloated-face guy, the one who looked drunk all the time, that had made it clear inside the bunkhouse. And now he lay dead in the sun outside it.

And the Stupid just kept coming. A Serrano man left the safety of the engine shack and charged the ditch, firing two .45s every which way. Milianos let him get up to the lip of the ditch, then shot him twice in the stomach so he'd fall in where they could get his guns. A cool head, that boy.

And since there was plenty of Stupid to go around, someone passed me a plateful.

And I gobbled it up.

"Trade me your shotgun for a carbine?" I asked Ray.

He just looked at me. Then unslung the shotgun from his shoulder. "What's on your mind?"

"The engine shack," I said. "That's the Serranos' strong point. If I can knock it out, Milianos will take the bunkhouse easy enough."

"What's on your mind?" Ray repeated and handed me the shotgun. I set it on its butt, muzzle up, and set my shotgun next to it likewise. They were loaded already, both barrels each.

"Back in the War, we would have thrown grenades at that engine shack till one of them landed inside." I picked up this-and-that from around the room and squatted by the scatterguns. "Maybe I can get the same effect..." I laid out four shotgun shells, broke them open with a hatchet, and poured their insides down the shotgun barrels. Ray was still watching outside, but he glanced my way and made a face when I emptied a box of carpet nails into the scatterguns. Someone had broke a bottle on the floor and I swept up the shards of broken glass with my hand and dumped them in, too.

"Tear some pages from a book for me, would you Ray?" He reached for one. "No, not the Conrad. Get the Emily Dickinson, that's good."

Ray wadded torn pages into loose balls and I stuffed them nice and snug into the shotgun muzzles so nothing would spill out. Next I grabbed some friction tape and had Ray tape the shotgun grips in my hands, with the butts good and tight along my wrists.

"How will you pull the triggers this way?" he asked, "Your fingers won't reach."

"If these act like every other shotgun I've ever seen," I got up and walked to the door, a rangy-looking idiot with a sawed-off shotgun at the end of each arm. "I won't need to pull any triggers. Now, do you think you can keep everyone's head down while I run from here to the engine shack?"

"I can if you don't stop on the way for a drink or something," He looked at my shotgun arms and gave me that ugly grin, "I hope you don't need to pick your nose."

"Shoulda thought of that before I taped up. Don't suppose you'd get it for me? The left one there, would you? No? Then if you'll just open that door and start shooting..."

"Good luck, Culley."

"Good luck, Ray."

Ray jumped out the door to a prone position and started firing the carbine.

And I started my run.

I'd known men to go crazy in the War, but I sure never thought I'd see old Vernon Culley shake the fruit tree like this. But there I was, sprinting across the road toward the ditch and the engine shack like bullets couldn't stop me. Ray shot sharp; the carbine was a good choice for the prone position since he wouldn't have to jack it like he would the Winchester. He nailed the bunkhouse first, firing at likely windows, generally drawing attention his way. Then he switched to the ditch, and I saw gravel fly up from the ground in front of me into the faces of the men from 'Nada. They all ducked, and what they thought of the sight of me, leaping over their heads like a long-arm baboon, is God's own guess.

Ray emptied the carbine while I was in mid-air over the ditch, and before I landed on the other side—which was mostly gravel, remember—he jumped back in the office, grabbed the Winchester, and started jacking rounds at the engine shack.

There's a trick to running across gravel, another handy item I picked up in the War: Soon as your left foot hits the ground, you swing your right foot in front. Then, before your left foot can sink into the loose stone, you pick it up and swing it in front of the right—which, if you've done it correctly, just landed in the gravel but hasn't sunk yet. You do that real quick—right-left-right-left—and it's like flying because you never really put your weight on any one spot, and because a man wasn't meant to travel like that—and won't for very long.

I did it long enough to hit the engine shack, though, and hunkered down between the vents so the men inside couldn't get at me. Not right away, anyhow. No one in the ditch was shooting at me now; they'd figured out what I was up to and begun firing on the bunkhouse to keep them from shooting me from in there.

While I caught my breath, I used my right forearm to cock the hammers on my left shotgun, and vice-versa. Then I inhaled deep, jumped up, raised my arms, spun, and stuck each scattergun into a vent slot, then slammed down—hard!

I didn't pull the triggers. Didn't have to. Gravity and the contrary nature of shotguns did all the work.

It happened. There was a god-awful roar and all four barrels went off at once, filling the inside of the engine shack with flying buckshot, burning powder, broken glass, carpet nails, and *"God gave a loaf to every bird..."*

And I'll say this: If I had it to do over again, I'd kick myself in the ass for even thinking of it.

CHAPTER 25

I guess things were kind of nasty for the crowd in the engine shack, but it wasn't much better for the idiot outside who touched off the shotguns. The recoil from four 12-gauge barrels firing all at once was like ...

... well, maybe when you fired a shotgun the first time, you held it too loose and the butt slammed your shoulder;

or maybe once you went off the high-dive and landed belly-smacker in the water;

or crossed the street and got hit head-on by a runaway truck.

It was something like that.

I felt myself jerked back by the arms, half deafened, and knocked spinning down the gravel slope before I even realized the guns had gone off.

Then there was just the feel of everything flying around my head in slow motion while I rolled downhill ass-over-belly-button.

I saw bullets slap into the side of the engine shack where I'd just been standing, and realized those ungrateful bastards from 'Nada must have opened fire on me soon as the blast went off. I wondered if they hit me.

Then I was looking up at empty sky.

Then down at a face-full of gravel.

Then back uphill as bloody Tony Serrano staggered out of the engine shack, shooting at the ground before he fell face-down all over it.

Then more sky swung into view, followed by a quick glance down-slope and another face-full of gravel.

I came to rest god-knows-where, half-covered with loose rock and all-covered with gray dust, and I decided to just stay there and listen to all the shooting and shouting somewhere back up the hill.

I kept at it a while, too.

Sooner or later, though, my mind cleared and I snapped out of it some. It occurred to me I was lying out in the open in the middle of a Mexican shoot-out, and I better get up and save my sorry hide. I rolled over, spat out a mouthful of dirt, blinked the sun out of my eyes, and looked around.

It was quiet. Damn quiet. I was scratched up, sore and dusty, and my left hand felt kind of tingly, but I was alive, it looked like. For now, anyway.

The shooting had stopped. So had the shouting. I looked up the slope. The only thing moving was two men, covered in gray dust and burnt gunpowder, and they were walking carefully down the gravel slope towards where I lay, which was somewhere near the bottom, between the storage shed and the privy. The man in front was the chubby-faced little

Diego who'd made a mess of scouting the engine shack, and he was carrying old Ernesto's long gun.

The other one was Milianos. He could see I was moving, but he didn't seem too concerned about it.

"Oh, my Blessed Virgin," Diego was saying, "can they all be dead?"

"I fear that is right, Diego," Milianos said gently.

"And my fault," Diego almost sobbed, "It was my fault..."

"I do not blame you too much," Milianos checked his guns and re-loaded them while they walked-slid slowly down the gravel. He was walking graceful and sure-footed in the loose gravel, but he was also gradually slipping behind Diego. "But I fear you will have this to answer for when we return."

"At least we-we got the bastards," Diego was bawling now, leading the way as he picked his way down toward me, "All but this one."

"That is true, Diego. All but this one," Milianos, walking easily behind Diego, holstered his guns and stopped dead-still.

He called, "Hey! DIEGO!"

Diego stopped and turned around.

And when the long barrel of that rifle was pointing to him—but not before—Milianos drew and shot Diego square in the chest.

I was right about Milianos: he was no back-shooter. That was his idea of handing out a fair chance.

Didn't do Diego much good, but it helped me out, because in the time it took Milianos to stop and kill him, I jumped in the privy. Milianos saw me do it and snapped a shot at my legs, but he was just too late.

When I say *I jumped in the privy* you have to appreciate that's a neat trick for a man lying in gravel with two shotguns still taped to the ends of his arms—could have gone on stage with an act like that, if I had a monkey—but I can be pretty amazing when I'm scared. And you should have seen me inside that outhouse, ripping the tape off my arms and unholstering the Harrington. Pretty inspiring stuff.

My left hand was kind of bloody, tingled like electric running through it some way, and that slowed me some, but no time at all, I had the familiar weight of that long-barreled .22 in my hand and peeked out the privy door, looking for Milianos.

He was nowhere in sight.

But the storage shed door hung open where it was closed just a second ago.

"You do fine work, Culley," Milianos' voice came from the dark inside, speaking Mexican now, "There's no one left but us—you and me."

"Thanks to you."

"A pity about poor Diego," his voice shrugged, "but he wanted to kill you. I saved your life."

"What about Ray? You save his life too?"

"No. I shot him down in fact. But that too was a mercy. One of the Serrano brothers was after him. The big one, I think. No difference, one of us would have killed him anyway."

There was a pause while I breathed the heat and stink of the privy and wondered if this would be the last place I ever lived. Then Milianos said, "Say, Culley, are you going to be in there a while? Because I sort of need to go."

"Come ahead."

"I will," he laughed, "and very soon."

There was quiet for a while. I liked that he wasn't going to insult me with promises or try to bargain when we both knew only one of us was going to sit down to dinner tonight. But I figured he wanted to keep me alive—if I wasn't too much trouble that way—till he found the Gold.

For my part, the storage shed was maybe fifty paces off, and I knew I could hit Milianos if I could see him and live to pull a trigger, but I also knew he shot just as straight as me and a damn sight faster, so in an even match, all the smart money would be on his side. Then I considered that he'd try to cripple me and that might slow his aim some, especially if I hunkered down. But I remembered I don't shoot good hunkered down, and besides I was sore from falling down the slope, and that might affect my aim.

Then I said the Hell with it, let's get stupid.

I jumped out—because I didn't want to die in an out-house – and charged up the slope towards the storage shed, sliding and twisting in the loose gravel, holding the Harrington in both hands out front, and firing every which-of-a-ways, two-hand: cock-then-fire, cock-then-fire... six shots. Wild shots, crazy-all-over-the-place shooting that didn't hit nothing but the air. Six shots.

Which left me three.

Then, about thirty paces from the shed, I dived prone on the ground. And while I fell, I rolled the cylinder back two notches.

I hit the ground hard and pulled the trigger twice more and heard the hammer "click" empty.

Twice.

That's all it took.

Milianos came swaggering out of the storage shed, grinning that lazy grin of his, and his guns were still holstered, he was that sure of himself.

The smug bastard.

I shot him three times in the left shirt pocket and he stopped smiling.

The first shot stopped him dead. And I mean that. The second shot hit and his right knee folded, just as the third shot jerked him left and spun him halfway around. He went down on his back and slid head-first down the gravel till he stopped in front of me, eyes wide open and mouth full of dust. Never even got his guns out. I was still prone myself, and I rolled over and looked him face-to-face, both of us lying there on that gravel slope but only one of us still breathing.

Damn.

CHAPTER 26

After a while I sat up, but I didn't feel like anything much. Couldn't figure out why at first, but then I realized I felt bad about Ray.

Kind of funny, that. It'd only been two-three minutes since Milianos told me Ray was dead and I missed him already. Still didn't feel like doing much. I scraped a place in the gravel to sit, felt around in Milianos' pocket, and found one of his rank cigars. Good job he kept them in his right pocket because those three .22 slugs I put there had torn his left pocket all too hell. I torched one up and took a deep drag.

The tobacco eased me down some, and while I smoked, I realized the sun was getting hard. I reached over and took the dead man's hat. It fit real good. I puffed some more on the cigar, felt a little better, and re-loaded the Harrington, knocking out the spent shells and feeding new ones into the cylinder. My fingers shook some, my left hand was getting stiff now, and bloody all over, but I got it done. Looked back over at Milianos lying there in the gravel.

Some way it didn't seem right. The big toothy bastard, he'd killed Ray, and all those men from 'Nada got killed likewise, and he'd planned on killing me even worse, and then he died fast and simple like that. I wanted to kill him again, just to even things up with the cocky low-life, and it bothered me I couldn't. Bothered me something fierce.

So that's where I was, sitting in the rocks, wearing a dead man's hat and smoking his cigars, not quite out of my mind but not far from it, when Otilio walked up behind me, slapped me on the back and laughed, "Eh! All is quiet, just as you said, *Commandante*. Did you leave the *gringo* alive for me? Where are the other—"

I turned around and pushed the Harrington into his belly.

You know, I didn't think nothing on Earth could cheer me up right then, but the look on Stable-Boy's face when he saw it was me—and I was sticking a gun in his tub—it gave me a deep-down smile, it truly did.

I saw a painting of Hell one time, and there was this one guy in the picture, a lost soul who just realized where he ended up and what was going to happen to him for the rest of eternity—and Otilio had that same look on his face.

And it made me laugh. A real laugh, a sick-sweet noise of pure pleasure.

I got up just as his knees gave out, and I stood over him, holding the gun and getting my laughing under control. Otilio wore two handguns on his hips, and I stripped them both off and tossed them *just* out of reach. Then I tore his hat off and slapped his face hard with it. And then slapped him again.

"Well, Otilio?" I asked in my best Spanish, "Why don't you ask *Commandante* Milianos if you can kill the *gringo* now?"

I swung Otilio's hat down at the big, dust-covered body. "There he is-" I whacked Otilio again with the hat. He just knelt there in the gravel and took it. "Go ahead and ask him!"

I was getting some real nasty ideas for this boy: thought I'd call to mind about his plans for me, make him recite them in detail, and fill in the parts he forgot. I wanted to make him say it over and over till his mouth dried, and I could kick the words out of him when he tried to swallow. And then I was going to really get started. "Ask him, Otilio!" I kicked him in the shoulder and tried to keep from laughing too hard. I swear it felt good as Christmas, what I was going to do to him.

Then I heard gravel come rattling down the slope and I looked up. Someone was limping our way, using Ernesto's long-gun to use as a crutch, and having a tough time of it, slipping and sliding in the loose rock.

"Ray?" I squinted in the sun, "That you?"

"A piece of me." He stumbled, caught himself, and got down to us some way.

"Milianos said you was dead."

"I guess you just can't trust a man like that." Ray bent forward to catch his breath. He glanced over at Otilio there on his knees and ignored him. Sat down, favoring his right leg.

I looked at Ray. Broken nose, split lip, swollen jaw, and a gash upside the head that almost closed his left eye. "He wasn't far wrong, from the look of you."

"I'm all right." He glanced over at Milianos' body stretched out in the dust. "Nice work."

"A dog always fights harder in his back yard." I sat down myself, next to Otilio, who was still kneeling, hatless. I handed his hat to Ray, who sniffed at it and put it on anyway.

"I could have used a hand with him if you weren't too busy," I said. "Where you been?"

"Got in a fight."

"Thought it might be something like that," I looked over his face again. "Who won?"

"Jury's still out."

I fished through Milianos' pocket and pulled out a cigar for Ray. Lit it off the end of mine. The tobacco on his split lip made him wince, but he puffed anyway.

"Big fellow," he said, "The one I fought with: big fellow."

"With a bad eye?"

"That's the one. You know him? Friend of yours?"

"Sounds like 'Cento Serrano," I said. To my right, Otilio started to relax, and he sidled just a half-hair closer to his guns. I gave him a hard look and he sidled right back again. "How'd you mix it up with big 'Cento?"

"Well it wasn't easy."

I guess back there, while I'm shooting the engine shack all to Hell, Ray's still in the office and he's using up the rest of the ammunition one way and another when all of a sudden Cento Serrano comes crashing through the door from behind and beats him near to death.

Ray knows a little about fighting, but he never saw anything as big as Cento, and that hurt leg slows him up considerable. He can't get his gun re-loaded. Can't get his hands around Cento's wrists (that's how big they are) for a good Judo throw. Can't even get past that big belly to grab hold of his neck. He throws every fancy punch he knows, and a few he just made up for this occasion, but Cento just squints his one good eye and starts pulling Ray's arms and legs off.

After some of this, Ray decides if he can't out-fight Cento he better out-run him. He gets loose someway and heads out the door. That's when he remembers he was shot in the leg. He gets about half-dozen steps to the closest mine tunnel, with Goliath right behind him, when his leg all of a sudden goes out and he hits the ground. Fast and hard. Which near as I can figure, that's maybe when Milianos thought he shot him.

Ray figures next thing he's going to get crushed or something, but Cento goes down right behind him—shot, maybe, or just playing possum like Ray, I don't know. But when Ray gets up running again, Cento he's up too, and right behind, and Ray makes it almost to the mine shaft before he falls again, rolling over, and Cento's just about on top of him now.

Which is right where Ray wants him. Cento's moving so fast he can't stop. Can't stop even when he all-of-a-sudden sees there's something in Ray's hands, and maybe he has time to wonder if Ray hit the ground again that second time just so he could grab that pick-handle and swing it like he's doing...

"He turned," Ray took a drag on his cigar, "but I still connected. Caught him in his one good eye."

"Good idea."

"I read it in that book last night. The part where Ulysses blinds the Cyclops. So you see the advantage of a good education. Anyway, Cento went running blind into the mine shaft." Ray stopped and took another drag on the cigar that used to belong to Milianos. He hawked, spit out a little blood, and swallowed a little more.

And I asked, "You finish him off?"

"I went back to the office shack, got hold of a coal-oil lamp and my .45, and went in after him." Ray nursed his split lip some. "But he'd fallen down a mine shaft maybe thirty feet."

"Dead, you reckon?"

"I sure hope so; I'm not going down to check, and he's too heavy to haul back up and ask him."

I threw away the end of my cigar and pulled another from Milianos' pocket. Got it going for myself, and Ray asked what went on down here and I explained how the lawman was a great shot but a lousy chess-player: I laid a trap for him yesterday shooting targets at the water-hole, and he walked into it today.

"What happened to your hand?" He pointed down at my left hand. I raised it and took a look. The end of my ring finger was mangled and twisted up like a dead candy-wrapper above the last joint, just smashed all up.

"I don't know." I studied the messy end of it. Didn't feel a thing. "Looks like the dog got it."

I figured later it must have got messed up by the trigger guard of that kicking shotgun, and when I come to look at it, I saw the hot barrel had seared it shut, mostly, so there wasn't much bleeding, but it sure was a mess. Didn't bother me a lot right then, but later on, it hurt like mother's tears.

Right then, though, Ray said, "Now what? I'm hungry." We stood up.

"Why don't you find us something to eat while I kill this dog?" I said it in Spanish and poked the Harrington at Otilio's head just for the pleasure it gave me to see his sick face. "Give me about twenty minutes—no, make it forty, I want to take my time with this."

"All right." Ray looked around. "I think there's food with the horses." He pointed to where Otilio had led the horses down to water at the drainage ditch. "Try not to make too much noise, will you? We don't want to spook the animals."

"I won't be making noise."

Ray limped off to the horses. I turned back to Otilio, gave him a big, friendly smile—and broke his nose with the gun-butt. He hit the ground with a solid, satisfying "*plop!*" and I cocked the hammer, trying to decide if I wanted to shoot his knees off first, or maybe his ankles so he could still crawl. The ankles seemed like my best bet... Then:

"Say Culley?"

It was Ray, limping back. The second time he'd stopped me doing this, come to think on it.

"Oh now what?"

"You aren't really going to kill him, are you?"

We were still speaking Spanish, and I said, "I sure am. And I figure to do it slow and painful enough, he'll remember it the rest of his life, which should be about lunchtime—" I gave Ray a level look. "—if I get started now and no one interrupts me too much."

"You're serious, aren't you?"

"Serious as sin."

"Well I wish you wouldn't."

"And why not?"

I'd been looking forward to this since the third time Otilio kicked me, back in that stinking cell in 'Nada, and I didn't feel like putting it off much longer. Irked me some, Ray spoiling my fun like that. "Is there some good reason not to kill this worthless pile? And have fun doing it?"

Ray sat down again and motioned me likewise. Otilio just crouched on the ground holding his bloody nose, looking from one of us to the other.

"For a start," Ray said, "If we kill him, who's going to take the horses back?"

I looked over at the dumb beasts. They'd drunk some, then moseyed to shade as much as their hobbles allowed. Otilio had done a good job with them.

"I got to admit that's a consideration, Ray," I said. "I hate as much as anybody to see an animal suffer. But if we lead them back up to the cliff-top and turn 'em loose, they ought to get back all right, most of them anyway."

"Maybe," he said, "but maybe not. And they'll certainly all get back if Otilio takes them. And along with them the bodies of these men. It will save us the burying."

"Burying?"

I could see now Ray's mind had got deranged by his ordeal, so I made my voice soft and reasonable. "Ray, these men were fixing to rob us as soon as they got through killing us—which would be right after Stable-Boy here got through cutting us up into little pieces to get the whereabouts of that Gold. Now I'm a forgiving man—I like to think so, anyhow—but I truly wasn't thinking to give them a big funeral or nothing."

"Still," Ray insisted, "it would be better to send back the bodies. Just those from 'Nada. Serrano's men we can drop down a hole, but these others, they have wives, parents, children who must know and bury their dead."

He went on, "Everyone thought they were going to get rich. They were going to make their families rich, build fine houses, a school perhaps. They spoke of it. Now, with them dead, the town of Quenada will die also. A town that size will not survive the death of twelve men. For those left in 'Nada, it's better they know it now."

He had a point there.

"Ray," I said, "you got a point there. And I'll admit it would be a fine thing for us to send this worthless dog back home with the remains of his friends and neighbors. But you know when he gets there, he's going to make up some story about how he killed all the Serrano brothers and we killed everyone else, and he'll say then we run away when his back was turned. When he gets through telling it, and word gets out, that's going to make Mexico kind of an awkward place for us, now ain't it?"

"Maybe," Ray nodded, wincing with the pain of moving his head. "But we're leaving Mexico anyway. And maybe he won't lie."

I just laughed. Then Ray got up—all stiff and hurting— and motioned me to one side where Otilio couldn't hear.

"You're right," he said, "but there is also this: I heard more talk. Otilio is married now to old Ernesto's daughter Ciera. The one in the cantina I told you of. And from everything I hear, he loves her well."

He looked me square in the eye, "She was good to me once; I would not make her a widow."

Well Hell, I thought, *There goes all my fun.*

CHAPTER 27

Before I get on to the next part, I need to say something. The way I told it back there, Serrano and his boys killed all the men from 'Nada—or Milianos did—and me and Ray didn't kill nobody but *banditos* and that bastard lawman. The way I told it, we didn't kill any innocent civilians and there wasn't any of the Serrano boys lying around afterward not-yet-dead or maybe-dying, and no hard choices left to make about it.

That's how I told it.

And that's how I'm going to tell it, too, because I ain't going to write down nothing that might jump up and bite me in the ass later on. But if anyone thinks it was that easy and that simple, well, they got a lot to learn about Gold, that's all.

We spent the rest of that day and part of the next resting up, cleaning up, bandaging up, and loading up. I picked through the bodies of Serrano's men. There were nine, all told: the three brothers and six hangers-on. It looked like

Paco Serrano had died first, which was his way of doing things—leading his boys right straight down Main Street in Hell. I picked through them, like I say, for anything useful, then tossed them down the pit with 'Cento while Ray worked on the ambulance and got the engine running again.

Hauling the Gold back up and loading it back in the ambulance was a two-man job, and I was working with a short hand while Ray had to favor his hurt leg, but it wasn't too bad—I'd seen to that when we hid it, remember, so we got it done, even with Ray's leg and my hand. That ring-finger was starting to swell, and it was ugly as damnation to look at till I picked up a used shotgun shell, stuffed some clean rag in the end, and stuck it over the whole mess. Fit pretty good and kept me from banging it too hard and cussing. I had plenty of antiseptic and bandages left in the Office, and one of the men from 'Nada had thought to pack some Laudanum, so we got along all right I guess.

Otilio had the job of getting his dead friends ready for freight, but at the end, Ray and I helped load them on the horses and tie them down good. While we were at it, I went through Milianos' saddle bags.

"Lookee here, Ray." I called him over to see what I'd found: Money, ammunition, a little food, what you'd expect for a ride like he just went on—but also other stuff: letters, old faded photographs, some Army papers saying what a fine job he did...

"It's like his whole life," Ray looked thoughtfully at one of the yellowed photographs, "I think this is his father,"

He picked up a stack of letters. "Looks like some woman wrote to him in the Army..." He ran a hand over a few old medals and trinkets. "It's as if ... maybe he knew he was going to die and wanted this with him."

"More likely he figured on leaving town permanently-and didn't want to leave all this behind."

Ray looked at me kind of surprised so I went on, "Now and then I used to collect some debts for Seamus Feeney back in Kansas City," I said, "When a man skips town, he packs up what's important to him—stuff like this: letters and pictures and such— and all the money he can carry. Even when he's expecting to get a lot more, he still packs up..."

And from the bottom of the saddlebag, I pulled out the Gold Bar—the one Ray walked through the desert with it taped to his leg.

"Maybe our old friend brought this along because he was sentimental about it," I said, "but my guess is he just wasn't planning on going back to 'Nada anytime soon."

Ray rubbed the side of his face, thoughtful-like. Then he noticed Otilio gawking over our shoulder at the stuff in Milianos' saddlebags.

"Do you still want to kill Otilio?" he asked in English.

"Don't toy with me, friend."

"All right," he smiled, "tell him to put that brick with the others."

It didn't make no sense, but I did as he said. Otilio was as puzzled as me, but he took the Gold bar and carried it to the back of the ambulance.

And I saw on Otilio's face what Ray had in mind.

The look he got when he opened the back doors and saw all that Gold, the smooth, heavy feel of that bar of it right there in his hands. Then having to put it in there with the rest and turn and walk away from the whole thing, away from Gold and back to hard work, horses and heat.

That look on his face was better than anything I could have put there with a whipping.

After that, I knocked some crates half-apart and arranged them over the Gold so if anyone opened the back of the ambulance it looked like just a load of machinery or something back there. I hammered them together tight then. Wooden crates are light enough to uncover the stuff pretty easy when the time comes, but for now it was pretty well hid. Then I looked around and took stock of things.

Ray and I were pretty well fixed. For money I mean. I picked near a hundred pesos off the bodies of the Serrano bunch, and I got even more than that off Milianos—yes, I robbed his body and it didn't bother me a bit—all that money in his pockets just made me more sure than ever that the cocky bastard was planning on lighting out with the Gold all along. But I didn't take anything off the other men from 'Nada.

Wanted to, but Ray stopped me.

There were more guns than we wanted to carry, so we ended up giving most of them to Otilio, that worthless pile of horse-hair, before he pulled out. Otilio got his horses with the dead bodies all lined up to go, but then Ray took him aside.

"Listen Otilio, and listen well. My friend says you will return to 'Nada and tell lies about us. You were going to kill us and take the Gold. You are lucky we leave you alive, but my friend Culley says you do not know gratitude. He says you repay mercy with treachery."

Stable-Boy insisted it just wasn't so, but Ray cut him short:

"Perhaps you may surprise me, but I do not depend on it. So before you go I want one thing of you. And this I will have."

Otilio just looked at him confused, and Ray went on,

"Otilio, I killed your brother. I took his life but I give you your own. In exchange for your life, you must forgive me that I took the life of Jorge."

Otilio's eyes widened.

"Forgive me, Otilio, for killing Jorge."

Otilio looked at him different. Hard to say how, but different. Then he said, "Heaven make you free of it. I forgive."

Then he mounted up, and that's the last we saw of him.

We got the ambulance going just fine, but my car, which the Serrano brothers had stole from me before the story started, was pretty much just a block of junk when I got it back—Paco Serrano never did grasp the concept of motor oil real good—so I left it back at Old Pesos. But not before I rescued the fifty U.S. Dollars I'd taped under the seat a few months back.

I'd got that money over the last couple years by selling off whatever I could, and some was left over from what old man Kurtz used to send down to buy equipment with. Now it was my back wages, and maybe fifty bucks wasn't much to show for seven years' work, but I was glad to get it. Back then, a man could live pretty good for a month or so on fifty bucks, if he was careful. Besides, I was still thinking to get a lot more.

The last thing before we left, I burned the letter from Biegel & Biegel. Ray asked me about it and I said I was dissolving a contract.

It was all closed up at Old Pesos Mine.

CHAPTER 28

I had to drive the ambulance because it hurt Ray's leg too much to work the pedals. After we'd gone a mile or so I asked him, "You happen to see who shot Paco Serrano?"

"To tell you the truth, I never noticed," he said. "Why do you ask?"

"Just strikes me funny some way." I let in the clutch and eased the old ambulance through the gears, getting the feel of it. "I didn't like him one bit. He was stupid and he scared me. Always scares me when there's somebody that stupid and he's running things. But I respected how he always got out in front when there was trouble."

"What's your point?"

"Didn't like Milianos either, and for the same reasons: he was stupid and he was running things. It scared me. But he handled himself real smooth, and he was no back-shooter. And the men back there, the ones getting carried back to 'Nada," I went on, "I had nothing against them. I even kind of liked that old guy who did the awful cooking."

"You mean Ernesto?"

"That's the one. Seemed like a thoughtful old cuss."

"What are you saying?"

"Some of these men was brave but stupid. Them from 'Nada, they were probably decent-enough folk. But the one man of the whole mess on either side who seemed completely worthless to me was Stable-Boy Otilio. And that's the only one who gets to go back home—Otilio."

"Life is funny sometimes."

"I'll write that down. Remind me if I don't get to it right away."

There was something else on my mind, but I wanted to ask about it real careful, and that spur road going back to the main highway took some attention driving. "I heard what you said to him back there. To Otilio, I mean."

"It seemed important."

"It gets you to Heaven with a clean slate then?"

"It clears the path, perhaps. I begin to think now I might make it." Ray took a drink of the Laudanum and it made him talkative. "When we first promised *Mijnheer* Ryckman to honor his contract, I truly doubted us. That we could do this thing."

"I doubted us too, you might remember."

"Yes," Ray sighed, "but it was you who showed me. What you said to *Mijnheer* Ryckman about seeking God's will. Not knowing it, but seeking to know it. That was the first part. And then we were riding back across the desert, and you talked of a man setting his priorities. You made me look at it all, all of it, and see for myself how it must be God's will for me to do this thing, God's will for us to keep our promise. And get to Heaven."

He looked out the window at the empty rockiness we were leaving behind us, then up to the road ahead. "Perhaps God sent you to show me this—to show me how it could be done. And now I begin to think we'll do it."

We bounced over a deep rut in the spur road, and Ray winced in pain from his hurt leg. I figured it must be cut pretty deep, but he just closed his eyes and said, "I begin to think this was God's way of saving me. Everything since I killed poor Jorge last year, it was all leading up to this, this chance for me."

"Seems kind of a roundabout way to get at it." I tried to slow down some and sound polite. "All those men from 'Nada and them dead now—that was God's will?"

"No Culley." Ray started to take another pull on the Laudanum, then changed his mind and corked the bottle for later. Didn't stop him talking, though. "A man decides for himself to go God's way or go his own. Last year, in a fit of anger I decided to kill Jorge and send my soul to Hell—but God showed me the way back. I decided to take that way. And I think now I may get there."

Yeah, maybe... I thought. "Seems you'll get to heaven anyway now Otilio forgave you. Ain't that how it works?"

"Otilio forgave me, but Otilio is not God." Ray made a short laugh-sound. "He's not even close. God will forgive me when I have kept my promise to a dying man,"

He looked at me. His eyes were kind of blurry, or maybe it was just the Laudanum, but his voice was funny when he said, "And thanks to you, I will keep that promise."

...And maybe not. Steering that awkward ambulance along the spur road was like pushing a barge over rocks, only not as much fun; it was slow to gear up and a little top-heavy on account of how we had to load the Gold on the sides; had to take the curves real careful-like, pulling on that heavy steering wheel with my one good hand, and I started telling myself that whatever I took for myself out of that Gold—maybe the whole thing, even—I'd earned it and earned it good. But all I said was:

"Just seems kind of raw to me, that's all. Them as died back there, most of them fought in the revolution, worked and sweated afterwards, and got nothing out of it—what they call *nada* down here. Then we show up with talk about getting rich and—" I slowed to swerve around another chuck-hole, hit a rock and Ray grunted with the hurting of it. At the same time, I banged my short finger on the steering wheel and cussed up something fierce till the pain went away.

"What I'm saying." When I could talk without swearing, I went on. "Is when a man's got nothing and sees a chance of getting rich, it seems kind of hard to say that's his own Free Will that makes him decide to take it. It's more like leading a thirsty horse to water, and it seems a hard kind of thing to send him to Hell for drinking."

Ray thought about that.

"Maybe they didn't go to Hell," he said finally.

"You think maybe not?"

"I hope not," he said, "I hope they went to Heaven. And that I shall meet them there where all is understood and all is forgiven."

Well that's just like a Christian: figure God makes the rules, but He's going to bend them up some and do whatever seems right. I never met God myself, but I've had to listen to a lot of folks who've spoke to Him and want to tell me what's on His mind—lots of them. And according to them, God hates the Germans. Or God hates the Jews and means for Germans to rule the world. A man I met once said God never meant for black kids to go to school with white ones—or Church, neither. God hates hard liquor and tobacco, but He figures snuff is all right. God likes to see folks getting married, but just once... or maybe to lots of women at the same time. God meant for Silent Cal to be President, and he gave us Herbert Hoover to pay for our sins. And one thing sure, God's letting all the Baptists get into heaven, and giving them the best seats.

Like I say, I've listened to a lot of people God has spoke to, and I've about decided that God means well, but He's one of these guys who'll tell you whatever he thinks you want to hear.

But I didn't see much point saying all this to Ray, and he was still talkative from the pain-killer:

"Don't you think much about going to Heaven or Hell?" he asked.

"Not much profit in it." I kept my eyes on the road while I talked. "I figure I've lived a good-enough life," I said, "I've always tried to help out my fellow man, if it wasn't too much trouble or when the pay was good. And I never went out of my way to hurt anyone that didn't need hurting—not real far out of my way, anyhow. So I figure I'll make out, I guess."

Looking back on it, if I'd been a Christian man that would have preyed on my mind some, since I was still trying to figure the safest way to kill this talkative cuss next to me and drive away rich.

See, I hadn't figured on both of us and the Gold all coming away from Old Pesos like this. Thought for sure Ray would get killed, or I would, and either way, I wouldn't have to worry about taking it all for myself, which I full intended to do. But with Ray and me both alive and carrying it all away, things was complicated.

I could see Ray sure-enough still meant to keep his promise to a dying man. Still meant to drive our cargo down to Guanajuato, sell it to this Spanish *Grandee* Samaniego as per contract, and bring the money back to Ryckman's widow. All of it. I didn't care much about promises to Ryckman, dead or dying, but Ray alive bothered me some.

For one thing, I didn't much want to kill him. Kind of liked him by now. But he sure wasn't the kind of man I'd leave alive to come looking for me if I run off with the Gold. No sir. If I wanted it—really wanted that Gold—I'd just have to kill Ray, that's all. Too bad about him going to Hell and all, but a half-ton of Gold ain't something I could just walk away from.

But I still wasn't keen on the idea of killing him. Not real keen, anyhow. For one thing, it wouldn't be the easiest thing I ever set about—a dozen men just tried it, and look how they ended up—and for another, I just didn't *feel* like it. Enjoyed talking with him, you know, and something about me, I hate shooting pleasant company in the back. It was quite a quandary, as the man says.

Then it struck me I didn't want the Gold. What I wanted was the money we were supposed to get for it from Samaniego down in Guanajuato. So I figured to wait till we got there and got the business end of things done, and then I'd get around to whatever I was going to do.

And I set it out of my mind.

CHAPTER 29

What with the new government highway all finished now, we should have made Guanajuato by late that night or early the next morning, but it ended up taking all of two days. That spur road was just too much for the tires on Ray's ambulance, so we lost time patching up, and then we had to head North—away from Guanajuato—back up the Highway to a little town called Tula, to get Gas and fix the tires proper.

Tula wasn't a bad little town. Maybe it was what 'Nada would have been if the government had built their brand-new road on that side of the desert. Not prosperous by a long ways, but not falling apart neither.

There was a garage there we could get the tires and gas, but that meant keeping close-by all the time to make sure the mechanic didn't look in the back too much. I covered up for it by saying we didn't feel good, which was true. Ray's leg was seeping and bleeding some, and I'd put that shotgun shell casing over my busted finger to protect it, but inside I could feel it throbbing hot. When I paid the man for gas and tires I gave him a little extra and asked was there a good doctor around anywhere.

He pointed us to a little place by the edge of town, and we drove up to where some old Indian woman was sitting out front of a little 'dobe two-room house, smoking a Meerschaum pipe and talking to some other old hag about the shapes of clouds off in the distance. They both looked like Methuselah's great aunt, especially the one with the Meerschaum, but I was glad to meet that talky Indian—I'd trust an old Indian over a school-educated Mexican doctor any day.

Ray and I both knew without saying it that one of us should stay by the ambulance while the other got doctored. He went in first and I sat down in the street, in the shade behind the rear bumper, with my back resting on the wheel and tried to forget about my throbbing finger. Looked up and down the street at nothing very much, because that's what there was to look at.

A couple doors down on the other side there was two gals looking out a window at me and the ambulance, fanning themselves and sweating.

Sitting there in the shade I tried not to be real obvious about looking back while they talked to each other, looked at me some more, then came out and stood in the doorway. Finally one of them came across the street, walking my direction while the other watched. Reminded me of those lizards back at the water hole, a dozen lives ago.

This lady sure didn't move like no lizard, though. She had an easy, loose kind of walk that made it pleasant to watch the black skirt slide over her bare legs. She wore a bright-colored print blouse, but her figure made it hard to tell just what the print was. I enjoyed the effort, though.

She just kind of wandered up by where I was sitting like she was passing this way anyhow, not looking at me exactly, but not looking away, neither. I forgot all about my finger and said in my best Spanish,

"Good day, Miss. And a lovely one, is it not?"

"Ah," She gave me a look like *Oh-who-put-this-man-here-?* and smiled a big white-toothed smile. It wasn't a pretty smile, really, but it'd been a while since I talked to a woman up close and I was glad to see they hadn't changed any. "It is warm, no?"

"It is warm, yes," I agreed, "But cooler here in the shade perhaps." I made a gesture to indicate she could sit down next to me if she wished; not an invitation exactly, but an opening.

"You are *Americano?*" she looked at the dusty road where I was sitting like she was considering whether it'd be worth getting her skirt dirty.

"I am German," I lied. I'd just had a hand in killing about half the male population of 'Nada, and I was kind of leery about giving my right name. I went on, "I am called Gunther von Gunther." Don't know if she believed me, but it relaxed her some more.

"You are on a long drive, perhaps?" She tried not to look too eager, but it wasn't hard to see she made her living off guys like me and was maybe looking for more business.

"We carry old weaving machinery from a worthless factory up north to a perhaps less worthless place to the east of here," I yawned, "Where they have promised to give us some small money for it."

"Ahhh," her smile got brighter, "You should come over to the *cantina*," She nodded her head across the street to where her friend was standing. "It is much cooler there. And there are drinks."

It sure didn't look much cooler, not the way her friend was sweating. And I've read too many stories in BLACK MASK to wander into a strange saloon in the company of shady ladies when I'm carrying a lot of money around. Still, there might be some way to work this...

"Alas," I sighed in my best Spanish, "And also alack. But I must wait here for my friend inside."

I made a sad face, then brightened and reached into my pocket for some of the money I'd lifted off Milianos. "But perhaps you could purchase four beers and bring them here. One for your friend, if she will be good enough to join us, and one also for my friend, eh? And perhaps something to eat?"

Her eyes got sharp and happy when I pulled out a couple pesos and handed them to her. "Just beer?" she smiled, "The tequila is very fine here."

"Just food and some beer," I smiled right back, "Four of them."

She took her time walking away, showing off some, and it was a sight worth showing at that, but she got back pretty quick with her friend, four beers, and a plate of something to eat.

"This is Lupe." She nodded towards her co-worker as she handed me the plate of food and one of the beers. I noticed she didn't offer me any change from those pesos, though. "I am called Margarita."

"There is a drink of that name." I opened the bottle by jacking it on the bumper, passed it to Margarita, took another one from her, opened it, and offered it to Lupe, who glanced nervously at Margarita before she took it. Finally, I got a pull on my own—warm, but not bad. Took my mind off my throbbing finger some.

"The drink called Margarita is tasty and intoxicating," I went on, "And it is served in a pretty glass."

She just smiled, but her friend Lupe giggled fit to bust and took a pull off her bottle that near-emptied it. Margarita studied the ground some like she was still trying to decide if it'd be worth the trouble to sit down next to me. Her friend Lupe looked like she'd be glad to raise her skirts and park it right there, but I guess professional ethics kept her from horning in on her friend's business. Or maybe she was just scared of Margarita.

"You will spend the night?" she asked, "Nice rooms at the *cantina*."

"It is a great misfortune." I made another sad face. "But we will most likely move on when we have seen this wise woman, and my friend—"

Just then Ray came out of the Indian woman's house, looking some better. His boot had been cut away at the top and there was a mostly-clean bandage above his ankle where Milianos' bullet had gouged him.

"—Ah, here is my friend now," I waved to Ray. "Hamlet, you must meet the ladies!"

I got to my feet and made a formal introduction, "*Senorita* Margarita, *senorita* Lupe, this is my good friend *senor* Hamlet."

Ray nodded and smiled. "Jose Hamlet," he said brightly, "From the town of Valverde." The girls looked up from me over at him.

You know, I'd plain forgot the effect Ray's face had on some folks. Forgot the way I'd felt back when I first got a load of that twisted ugly grin of his. I guess it surprised me when I glanced over at the gals to see their faces. They didn't scream or look away or nothing like that—just kind of gave him a look like he was somebody's dog. The look was there-and-gone, replaced in a half-second by professional smiles, but it was there and I seen it.

Well maybe I was tired and grouchy from the trip, or maybe my hurt finger bothered me more than I knew of, but something about that set me off. Felt myself go all over angry and the next thing I knew someone had almost smashed my beer bottle against the ambulance. And it was me, I'd just about snapped and done it.

Caught myself in time, though. Calmed down and slowly blinked the red out of my eyes. No sense calling a lot of attention to us right here. No sense wasting beer, neither. I drank off the rest of mine and turned to Ray, who was already sipping at his. "That old bag in there any good?" I glanced down at Ray's leg.

"She seems to know what she's doing." Ray took a drink of his beer and looked around. "Anyone who practices medicine in a small town like this has to be pretty good at it. Word gets around when everyone lives close. Anyway, the place is fairly clean and her knife is sharp. She'll talk you to death, though."

"I thought Indians don't talk much."

"Hah!" Ray gave me his twisted grin. The girls were enough used to it not to look away. "I guess you never lived on a reservation, eh?"

"Guess not."

"There's plenty of talkers and she's one of them. Get her to tell you about General Crook."

By now Lupe had got clear over her first reaction to Ray's face and she looked like she'd like to talk some with him—about current events or trends in modern literature maybe—and she was smiling at him just the same as she had me. So was Margarita.

Well, fine then. I was all simmered down now and wondering what got me so mad in the first place. I turned and went inside the medicine woman's 'dobe shack.

CHAPTER 30

I t was a low-ceilinged two-room place, mostly dark, with a little pot of water boiling in a small fireplace. I liked that she knew about clean water.

"My friend says you are a wise woman of medicine," I said in Spanish.

"You're American." Her voice sounded like something from a dusty old trunk, and her English was like an old family bible you keep wrapped in tissue and bring out on special occasions. "Me too. I like to talk 'Merican."

"That right?" I tried to forget my throbbing finger and look fascinated.

"Your friend hurt that leg some."

"Yeah," I said, "Hunting accident."

"Hunting accident." Nothing showed on the old bag's leather face. "He also said that. Siddown there."

I sat down on a solid-looking wood chair at a small, clean table.

"How you hurt that finger?"

"Mechanical," I said, "Went to fixing up that truck and got stupid with the fan belt."

"That happened too, I guess. Lessee." She sat down across the table from me and looked at the shotgun shell I had jammed over the end of my ring finger, but she didn't touch it, just looked at the red swelling showing under the edge. "Hurt much?"

"Like Billy-be-Jesus."

She cleared her throat with a noise like a mine shaft collapsing. "Mmmm." She nodded, pointed at the shotgun shell. "Good idea, that. You take him off then. I don't touch it. You drink Laudanum?"

"When I can get it." I took my time working the shell off the end of my finger, tugging real gentle at it, first one side, then the other. But it still hurt like I'd stuck it under a train wheel. Smelled bad, too, once I got the wrapping off.

The old woman looked at it close while she talked, "Bad stuff Laudanum. Kills hurt, kills brain, kills the man who drinks it someday. But for bad hurt you gotta get some."

The finger was red-hot and swollen most of the way, but above the top joint, it was cold and kind of greenish-looking. She still didn't touch it. Finally, she said. "You got any more? Laudanum?"

"I think my friend drank the last."

"Too bad," she nodded, "This gotta come off. The end there. At the knuckle. Gotta cut him off."

"I Kind of thought so too." I looked at it, feeling the beer start to churn in my stomach. "You going to do it?"

"You gonna let me?"

202

"Nothing else for it, I guess."

I leaned back in my chair and laid the hand across the table toward her side. "I'll have to look away when you do it."

"Okey-dokey."

"And I might scream and struggle some."

"Okey-dokey."

She rose and picked up a big meat cleaver and a bottle of some kind of alcohol. Started talking around some, like this was no big deal. "From Arizona I am." She checked the edge on the cleaver with her thumb. "Yah! Plenty sharp."

"My friend says you knew General Crook."

"Hah!" Her face wrinkled up even more, like that was a pretty good joke. "Little kid from Arizona I lived. Lived on reservation some. Went to Mission School. Good school. I liked it. Good teacher. Sometimes there a doctor comes, I help him some, good job. But reservation stinks. Stinks bad. Nothing there much. I got tired of all-the-time nothing."

She walked over to the fire and poured alcohol over the blade. "One day a bunch of talk on the reservation, the young bucks gonna ride out and take back our land. Take back the wholedamn country. I think I'm gonna ride with them. Ain't gonna stay there with them damn blanket squaws. Gonna ride, I am. Young bucks and me broke into the store. Burned the school. Killed the teacher. We're just children then. Stupid children."

She stuck the alcohol-soaked cleaver into the fire. I Watched it burn with a small blue hissing flame, then glow shiny. Seemed all at once like everything I ever ate was sitting there in my stomach again while she talked on:

"Long time back this was. Stole horses and joined up Geronimo. Chiricahuas tribe he was. Big stuff. Sleep outdoors, ride all day, steal cattle, burn houses. To the bucks I'm just like one of them. Good life till General Crook comes."

She set down the cleaver a minute so she could fish a hot ember from the fireplace with a pair of tongs and put it in an earthenware bowl. Then she carried the bowl, the alcohol, and the cleaver back over to the table.

"General Crook," the old bag was saying, "He come along with a few many troops and couple hundred Apache. Chase us clear down to Sierra Madres."

I tried to forget about that meat cleaver and concentrate on what she was saying. General Crook went after Geronimo back in 1883, more than fifty years ago now.

"Apache beat us good," she was droning on in a dull, sing-song voice, kind of relaxing, I guess, "Whip us good. Take our food, horses. Geronimo surrenders, but I don't wanna go back some. The ghost of that teacher maybe still up on the reservation watches for me. And the place stinks. I don't wanna go back."

She poured a little more alcohol over the blade and held it close over the hot ember in the bowl. I smelled the alcohol burning off, started to get kind of dizzy.

"I come down here," she grinned, "Easy for me to slip away, they see me all they see is some blanket squaw or a Yaqui woman mebbe. I come here. Work for doctor down here. Big fool but smart man. I learn smart stuff, forget foolishness. Someday he dies, now I'm doctor."

She gently took the fingers of my left hand and made a fist of all but the ring finger, which she left sticking out from my fist, front-down on the table so I couldn't curl it up all of a sudden. Hurt like Christ on the cross.

She reached over slow, grabbed the wrist of my tensed-up left hand, and held it tight down on the table. I couldn't take my eyes off the black, twisted end of my finger poking out on the smooth wood surface.

All of a sudden, the old woman looked over my shoulder, out towards the open door behind me. Her eyes narrowed and got a scared-angry look on her wrinkled face.

"What wrong your friend?"

I half-spun in my chair, forgetting her grip on my wrist.

Through the open doorway, I could see the ambulance just sitting there and hear Ray talking with the ladies, calm and pleasant. Nothing going on at all. Then:

THUNK!

The sound came from the table. I felt kind of an electric shock shoot up my arm, then a cold-hot-cold-hot sensation of burning. Smelled searing flesh and it was mine. I spun back around. The old woman had lopped off the end of my finger and was holding the hot edge of the cleaver over the stub to seal off the wound, still clamping my wrist to the table with her strong right arm.

I'm not sure what it was that happened then, but I'm just glad I come out of it before anybody got hurt. I felt myself go all-over red-angry, and I called the Indian an old bitch and went for my pistol with my free right hand. Next thing I knew, the meat cleaver was edge-up about an inch from my throat, and the old woman was giving me a look like, *You want to think this over a minute?*

I felt the hate-crazy drain away from me like water pouring off. My knees went out on me and I sat back down fast, dizzy and sick. The old woman let go my wrist and put a slop-bucket in front of me and I filled it with the beer I'd just drunk, along with most of everything else back to a week or more. Finally finished and looked up.

"Thanks," I said.

"Welcome," she answered like she'd just held the door for me or something.

"No." I tried to shake the dizziness out of my head. "Thanks for not killing me."

"Welcome," she answered again, like she'd just held the door for me or something.

"Don't know what come over me there." I was starting to get that sour-gack throwing-up taste in my mouth, and looked around for something to drink.

"Some dam Injun cut off your finger, you got mad." She smiled wide and cackled, "Good trick, huh?"

Still using the meat cleaver, she cut open a lemon, squeezed the juice into a cup of hot water, and spooned in some sugar. Handed it across the table to me and I drank it down quick. Then she brought another bowl of water—cold water—to the table and stuck my finger in it.

"Take away the heat, it don't burn so bad," she explained, "How the stomach?"

"Fine."

"Sure, sure." She got busy over at a shelf by the fireplace, cleaning off the meat cleaver and picking through some stuff. "How do that finger feel now?"

I pulled my finger out of the water and saw it was now about as long as the little pinkie next to it. Didn't hurt just then, but I was scared to move it or touch it.

"All right, I guess."

"Mmm-hmm."

She turned back around to me with some white rags in her hands. "Gonna hurt like damnation and hellfire pretty soon by tomorrow. Fix you up for now." She brought over a real small earthenware jar with some kind of salve in it, smelled like the stuff she put on Ray's leg. "Stick in the finger."

I stuck my finger in. It was cool and took away the pain some. Not much, but some. She handed me a strip of white rag. "Wrap him up. Don't use too much bandage. Gonna swell."

While I wrapped up the gooey-salve-covered end of my finger she picked up the empty shotgun shell I'd had over it when I came and pushed a dab of that smelly glop up inside of it.

"Good idea," she smiled down at the shotgun shell like it was Edison's light bulb and handed it back to me. "Put him on."

I slid it snug but gentle over my shortened finger. It fit good. I could feel the throbbing inside, but this looked promising.

"You got no more Laudanum huh?" she asked.

"'Fraid not." I tapped the shell-covered finger gently on the table and decided real quick not to do that any more than I had to.

"Too bad," she picked up a leather pouch and pulled out a couple dried roots that looked like potatoes from Hell. "You gonna want Laudanum. Too bad. Chew on this stuff. Chew him with sugar. Awful taste, sugar helps some. Not much. Eat something first."

"This takes away the pain?"

"Not much. Some, though." She picked up her pipe and looked around for tobacco. Then she spotted a squashed bug on the table. "You want him?"

I looked down at the squashed bug and saw it wasn't a bug at all—it was the end of my finger, black and dead, just lying there on the table.

"What the Hell I want that for?"

"Some folks keep it. Think you can't go to Heaven unless the whole body goes with you. They carry it around for years sometimes."

Well outside a church, I'd never seen so many folks so bothered up about getting to Heaven as lately. Damn lot of aggravation, you ask me. I felt a tingle on my face and it suddenly struck me the red-angry was coming over me again. I took a deep breath and made it go away. But not before I batted the bit of finger off the table and into the fire. It burned with the same sickening smell as when the old woman seared my finger, and I felt my guts jump again, but I got it under control. The anger was all gone now, but *Watch that*, I told myself again, *Just better watch that angry stuff*.

"What do I owe you?"

She didn't look surprised, exactly, just blinked, like no one ever asked her that before.

"Why? You got *pesos*?"

I just almost grinned at that. "A couple *pesos*."

I reached into a pocket and pulled one out, handed it to her respectfully. "Not much, seeing how you held off killing me like that, I guess."

Her wrinkled face wrinkled a little more, into kind of a sad grin. "Yeah, that starts hurtin' tomorrow you gonna curse some old Indian bitch bones."

"Got something else for you." The idea hit me sudden-like. "Come out here."

Out on the street, Ray was sitting on the dusty ground drinking beer, eating *frijoles*, and getting the ladies drunk on tequila.

"Looks like you found a wife," I said, "Two wives maybe."

"She's young yet, and not much for intellectual conversation." He hugged Lupe playfully with one arm and she broke out laughing again, "But I believe she could sing Polly-Wolly-Doodle all day."

He held up a plate to me. "You want something to eat?"

My stomach lurched at the sight of it, but I made myself take some. Chewed it careful and swallowed it slow. It stayed down.

I turned to the Indian woman. "Hungry?"

She shook her head.

I turned back to Ray. "I thought I'd offer the good doctor here a hunting rifle for all her work."

"That's a fine idea," Ray got to his feet—carefully—handed me the plate, and opened the side door on the ambulance. Margarita and Lupe tried to get up, too, but they made such a mess of it, it struck them funny and they sat down laughing again.

Ray turned to the Indian woman, with Tony Serrano's hunting rifle in his hands.

"We cannot pay you what your good service deserves," he said politely in Spanish, "But I hope you will take this with our thanks."

She looked at Tony Serrano's gun with something like respect. Took it in her left hand and ran her right hand along the shiny barrel and polished stock. Then she snapped it to her shoulder with one fast, smooth motion.

"Killer-rifle," she lowered it carefully, speaking Spanish a damn sight more fluent than her English. "It whispers in my ear of taking many lives. A thing to be cherished or destroyed. I will have to keep this many years to work the evil out of it and make it fit for the hands of men once more."

She smiled at me and switched back to English. "Rifles like this, me and Geronimo would still be up in the Sierra Madres, laughing down at General Crook and them damn Apache."

"Probably so," I said.

"Maybe not," she grunted. "*Muchas Gracias.*"

"*De nada.*"

Ray and I turned to get back in the ambulance, and the two women finally got up and made it over to a bench on the sidewalk, still laughing, and then Margarita, I guess it finally occurs to her we're going, and she gets her laughing stopped for a minute and she says to me:

"You leave without seeing the other German?"

CHAPTER 31

I looked at Ray and he looked right back at me.

I smiled casually at Margarita, "Another German, Honey?"

"*Si*, he waits in the *cantina* and asks of you," she turned to Lupe, like as if to back up her story, and something about the sight of her friend got her giggling again. Which started Lupe going, and the next second they were both falling off the bench, laughing fit to kill and too drunk to get up. Or answer any more questions about Germans.

"Ahh, Culley." Ray looked down at them. "The love that might have been, eh?"

He looked hard over at the *cantina*, across the street and a few doors down, as far into the darkened windows as he could. Like most places in that part of the country those days, the windows were open. No glass or screen or anything to keep someone inside from watching us out here. Or shooting if he felt like it. Ray opened the passenger door on the truck and slid in easy-like, and as he sat down, he pulled the carbine from behind his seat.

"Just nothing to do I guess, except-" I stepped over the drunken whores in the street, which set them laughing even harder, gazed regretfully down at them, "-pick up the tattered pieces of my life and move on," and walked around the truck to get in, real casual-like.

I looked over at those open windows and the dark-shadowed inside as well as I could myself, and didn't see no more than Ray had, then slid under the wheel and snugged the Harrington over to my left side so it would hang off the end of my seat for an easy cross-draw, loosened the flap on the holster, "I don't figure anybody'd shoot us here in the middle of Main Street."

"Maybe not." Ray looked wistful-like. "This could be somebody else. Not our Nazi at all."

"Yeah, maybe someone else's Nazi," I said, "And maybe he's got friends with him."

"I guess we'll see once we get moving."

I reached behind my seat and pulled out a box of shells for that rifle we gave the old woman that cut off my finger. She was standing close, watching like someone who knows there's going to be a fight, and maybe one worth seeing.

I handed her the shells. "You feel like doing a favor?"

She grinned wide as a jack-o-lantern but not as pretty, and slid three shells into the magazine of Tony Serrano's old hunting rifle. Chambered one round, then slid in three more.

"Feel like old times!" she cackled.

Sitting there behind the wheel of that truck, short-fingered, half-sick, and all-scared, I couldn't help but to grin at the blood-thirsty look of her.

"We're heading out," I said, "If a man comes out of that *cantina* and points a gun at us, would you maybe stop him from doing that?"

"I maybe shoot somebody's head off his shoulders and it rolls down the street. Okay?"

I got to say, she was a doctor to give a man his money's worth.

"Okay?" she said again like she was hoping I'd ask her to charge into that *cantina* and burn it to the ground. And anyone in it. "Anything more, too?"

"You got a good-luck spell?" I asked.

Her leathered face turned dark.

"Lucky spell? For little children," she spat, "I don't believe it. You don't believe it. You stupid?"

"No." I looked down at the whores sitting in the road, still laughing fit to kill. "Not stupid, just greedy."

Once we got moving and couldn't see the *cantina* any-more—and hadn't heard any hell break loose behind us—I breathed a little easier.

"So he doesn't shoot us in the middle of Main Street."

I worked the gear shift some, picking up speed as we headed south out of town, and winced with the pain of using my left hand on the steering wheel.

"Doesn't have to." Ray angled the back-view mirror on his side so's to look out behind us. "Lots of open country between here and Guanajuato."

A little time passed while I thought that over and put some miles behind us.

"Maybe he knows where we're headed," I said, "but if he don't, he'll figure us to double-back north."

"That's what I'm hoping," Ray said, "He'll head north and – oh Hell."

He saw it in the mirror on his side before I did. A small black dot behind us on the highway, in the mirror no bigger than a fly. Getting bigger fast, though. And nothing to do about it but push the pedal down and hang on.

Along that stretch south of Tula, it was good flat packed-gravel highway, running in gentle curves around dunes that got taller and wider the further we went. Good road for speed. I opened her up to see what she'd do.

What she'd do was fifty miles an hour, the engine screaming like a cat got caught in the crankcase. And the damn thing was still top-heavy and unsteady when I took the curves. I eased it down to forty, which helped some, but it helped the black dot behind us, too.

They don't dig drainage ditches alongside the road down there because it don't rain enough to make it worth the effort. Every time there was a bend in the highway, this black dot went off the road on the inside to cut the corner, gliding up over the dunes, raising plumes of dust behind him, getting closer, till I could see it was what I expected: a little man on a big motorcycle.

"He handles that machine like he's had some practice." Ray spoke loud over the rush of air coming in the windows and stared in his mirror.

"Wonder if he shoots as good as he drives."

"I'll let you know in a minute. He's getting a gun out." Ray had the carbine out now, but he didn't go sticking his head out the window none. Which was a good thing, because the German took a shot just then, and it banged off the door on his side, just above the handle. My ears rang with the ugly *"snap!"* of it.

"How far behind us?" I could hear the deep, self-important *"sput!-sput!"* by now, and I didn't like it much, how close it sounded.

"Twenty, thirty feet maybe." Ray tried to keep his head down and angle himself to see better, and his face twisted up with the hurt on his leg.

"Hold on to something." I swerved the ambulance half-off the road on his side, just enough to raise a cloud of sand behind us. Soon as the dust come up, Ray leaned half out his window and fired a couple rounds into the dust. Then he got back inside in a hurry as the German pulled up closer through the cloud and shot off his side-mirror, then dropped back again.

"Seems like he shoots pretty good, too." I just had time to say it when the German showed up in my side mirror. I caught a glimpse of that big, nasty-looking long-barreled Mauser, the folding stock cradled in his shoulder. Then a bright muzzle-flash and the mirror flew clean off.

"Damn!"

Didn't seem like much else to add, as that just about summed up the situation. I couldn't see behind me anymore; just hear the noise of that big old motorcycle engine getting closer.

"He's coming up on my side, Ray."

"Where I can't get a shot at him."

"Get ready." I swerved left, hard and fast, and heard the motorcycle noise drop back sudden. Then I went left a little further, and Ray leaned out for another shot, then back inside as two more rounds cracked into his window frame. I swerved over thataways, then back left, raising lots of dust behind us.

"Maybe I can suffocate him."

Just then I felt the sick, sluggish feel of tires starting to sink into the sand, felt us slow up as the wheels spun, and I got back over to the road quick as I could.

"Good idea while it lasted," Ray said.

The German was back on my side of the ambulance now, coming up fast. I swerved again, but he just swerved wider, staying on my side. And still coming up, not behind anymore, but damn near beside of me. A round went clean in through my open widow and out the roof in front of me.

Well, only one thing for it.

"Real tight now." I went straight off the road, and up a dune, not swerving, but straight up.

"Hang on."

Drove right upwards on the hot sand with that motor-cycle *sput-sput!* louder in my ear, then angled left just a little.

I couldn't see the German, but I could hear his infernal engine, feel it getting closer, right alongside now, as we went cross-ways up the dune, and I felt the wheels start to sink in the sand, slowing us up all of a sudden, and the

German coming up alongside, maybe faster than he figured, probably drawing a bead on my left ear...

I cut left fast as I could and the top-heavy ambulance
did the rest.

We went tipping over sideways.

On purpose.

There was a giddy, swimming-in-air rush as the floor
swung up underneath me, the noise of Ray banging into
something and swearing, the strain on my arms and the
pain of it as I held hard onto that steering wheel while we
tipped clean over. And then just the sick, satisfying *crunch*
of the side of the ambulance mashing the German underneath it. And a *slam!* as the load in the back shifted and half
a ton of Gold pounded him down into the sand.

CHAPTER 32

What with one thing and something else, it was late afternoon the next day when we drove onto the ranch of Don Escachza de Samaniego, a ways outside Guanajuato, and pulled up in the courtyard in front of his fine hacienda.

It wasn't all that hard getting the ambulance back upright. After it buried the German it slid down the dune with the wheels at the bottom, which gravity will do for a truck when you've got a half-ton load in the bed. It was just a question of unloading the Gold, scooping sand out from underneath the chassis till it righted itself, then stacking the Gold back and slapping the crate together around it again.

Oh yeah, and loading up the dead German. Him too.

Ray figured we were still pretty close out from a town where they didn't get a whole lot of visitors, and if that German's body turned up so soon after we left, somebody might start looking to ask us about it. I wanted to just bury him in the sand, but Ray said the wind was tricky in those parts, and I had to agree. We ended up packing him along with us in the back of the ambulance, behind the Gold. Gave me a good excuse to go through his pockets for loose change, too.

Hot and thirsty work, though, and it didn't do my short finger any wonders, neither. Ray had thought to stock up some beer, and we drank it and chewed on that awful-tasting root the old Indian witch gave me, and it helped some I guess.

Once we'd washed the dust out of our throats and got back on the road, we talked some, and it was a pleasure to talk with a man educated like Ray was. We'd get on to some book we'd both read, and somehow he'd got something out of it I'd missed.

You take HAMLET, for instance: I had to read it in college, and all I got out of it was sleepy, but Ray:

"You never saw it on a stage?" he asked me, "You just read it out of a book?"

"And took a test about it, yeah."

"There's your problem," he said, "It wasn't written to be read, it was written to be acted out. I saw it in a theater in San Francisco, and three times on an army base when a traveling show came through, and I'd watch it again any time."

"I never could figure out why it took that king so long to get around to killing Hamlet," I said, "Took me near a week to read as far as that last act."

It came back to me again just then, what the teacher said to me all those years back ago, about HAMLET and how my soul wasn't equal to the task. I didn't mention it to Ray, though. Just took another sip of beer and wished I had something cool to put on my hurt finger.

While we drove and talked, the countryside changed from desert to something softer and greener, with miles and miles of clear open all the ways around. And after a while it got plain to see we were on somebody's land. No fences, nothing like that, just the dirt road was better kept-up, no dead branches or range-litter lying about, and if you looked around, it just seemed like somebody paid attention to things here.

Rancho Samaniego, when we spotted it, was a fair-sized place, solid-built of adobe and cut stone, homey-looking but not too fancy, and the men working the ranch looked clean and dependable. We'd been driving on this property for several miles before we drove through a big stone archway into a wide courtyard to get to the *hacienda*. I looked around at the neat stone walls, the fat animals and clean laundry flapping on a line a ways off, and I figured Don Escachza de Samaniego must be a good man to work for. Looked forward to doing business with him.

Ray and me had run out of talk and started singing to pass the time. Getting his leg shot up hadn't improved his voice none, but he knew all the words to *"Red River Valley"* and he sung it like he meant it. I joined in, and folks say

I carry a tune like I meant to kill someone with it, but we managed,

"... *But remember the Red River Valley,*
And the cowboy who loved only you."

Mournful, it was.

We'd just finished the part about sweet-words-she-never-would-say when we reached the front of the *hacienda*, climbed out of the ambulance, and an old woman came out the wide oak front door to see what we wanted.

Ray told her we had business with the Don, and she replied that Don Escachza de Soto de Sotomayor Samaniego was unavoidably detained for a time, but he would see us in an hour or so if we cared to wait. That seemed kind of hinky to me. I said we'd discuss it.

"When I think about it Ray," I said in English, "seems to me we just now drove across a big long stretch of nothing-much to get here. If Samaniego is gone, where the hell is he that he could get back in an hour or so?"

"And if he's here on the ranch." Ray finished my thought. "Why can't someone just go get him?"

"Probably some real good reason," I said, "but just the same I think I'll strap on my gun. Want yours?"

"Thanks. Hand me both of them if you would." Ray explained to the nice lady while he buckled on his .45s that our business should not wait, and I slid my holster over to the left side, but the hardware didn't impress her none. She just nodded and stood there.

Ray said Samaniego was expecting us urgently. More nodding and standing. Finally, Ray told her to go inside to whoever was in charge right now and mention the name Ryckman, and that finally got her moving.

Which was a good thing for her, getting out of my sight, because my short finger was paining me some and I could feel myself turning nasty. Got to wishing I'd kicked Otilio around some more, back when I had the chance, or maybe mashed the dead German a little flatter.

Pretty quick a man came out, middle-age, slim, and short but capable-looking, in one of those fancy-trimmed jackets they wear on formal occasions. He said he was glad we were here, and Don Escachza de Soto de Sotomayor Samaniego was glad we were here, and he would join us presently, but meantime please come into the kitchen for some food and drink.

The kitchen, mind you. Not the living room or dining room, where they'd greet guests. That rankled me. I started to tell him like Hell we were leaving the truck alone with a bunch of thieving dirt-wallowers, or something like that, but Ray checked me:

"My friend and I are weary," he talked Spanish, "We have come some little distance and at some small trouble to ourselves. All in order to fulfill a contract with Don Escachza. We may not leave our responsibility, which is carried in this ambulance. Imagine our distress to find your worthy employer will not receive us."

"But it is not so," the other protested politely. "Don Escachza de Samaniego is most pleased you are here, and he wishes to conduct business with you presently," He glanced to the West, "Don Escachza will greet you personally in perhaps half an hour. Until then please accept some refreshment."

He had someone bring out beef, beer, and *tortillas*, and he insisted on setting up a big wood table and chairs for us out there in the courtyard. We ate some, but I didn't feel real good about it. Down there they don't get a lot of company, and they have a code of hospitality: when someone comes by, they usually set him down in the dining room to a good meal with the family—like treating him well was a point of honor.

But we'd been told to go to the kitchen. And the little guy in the fancy jacket hadn't said anything about accepting their hospitality, like you'd normally expect. All he said was that Don Big-Boss *"wished to conduct business"* with us.

Nossir, not a good sign at all.

When the Sun got down to the horizon, Fancy-Jacket lit torches and lanterns, and then Don Escachza de Samaniego appeared in the doorway. He looked every inch the Spanish Grandee: tall, fat, straight as a ramrod, with a big nose and chin, steel-gray hair, and a mustache like a black rubber hose. He was all dressed up in his Sunday best as he strode out to the table where we'd been picking at the food, the dust kicking up on his shiny boots.

"Visitors!" he barked, "We have visitors! Gonzales, why was I not told? How long have you kept the gentlemen waiting thus? Please—" He waved an arm. "Please gentlemen, come inside."

I noticed he didn't call us guests—*invitados*—he used the Spanish word *visitantes* for "one who visits" which ain't the same thing as a guest. And he'd invited us in, but he hadn't said anything about accepting his hospitality. Those are big differences down in those parts, and I figured this was my chance to make the speech about Like Hell we were leaving the truck, but Ray stopped me again.

"It is you, Don Escachza, who must pardon our rudeness. It pains me and my friend also to decline your invitation. We are regrettably on a mission of sacred trust, and we dare not leave what has been entrusted to us."

A look flickered across the old man's face, like we'd just knocked his hat off. It was there-and-gone—just like the look those whores gave Ray—and then he was all smiles again. Just like the whores.

"The blame is upon me for keeping servants who delayed you in such unseemly fashion," he insisted, "But your duty to this mission, deserving of praise, is now completed. Your mission has ended once you have reached my land. The responsibility for the transaction now is upon me and-"

I turned my back on him, went to the ambulance, and pulled out Ryckman's contract. It was getting darker and kind of chilly out, but I was burning too short a fuse to notice as I walked back and stuck the papers under his big nose.

"I think it says here you pay us now," I said as level as I could.

Again, the look from Don Escachza like I'd tracked mud in his church. And it lasted a little longer this time, the look did. Guess he wasn't much used to folks turning their backs when he talked. But he took the papers and scanned them quickly, like they were a copy of something he'd seen already. Then he looked at Ray—not at me—with his eyebrows raised in question.

"You have it there? The Gold?"

Ray took him around back of the ambulance, swung open the back doors, and raised the tarp. While I watched everyone else, he picked up a tire iron and went after the loose-nailed crates I'd slapped around the Gold. Just tore them to pieces. Then he set a lantern on the bumper to light what was inside.

I heard a quiet gasp blow across the courtyard. That was the first I noticed that four or five ranch-hands had joined Don Escachza and the steward Gonzales. But everyone just stared at the Gold like it was Baby Jesus himself in the back of that truck, smiling and waving at the crowd.

A long moment passed.

"You have done well," Don Escachza said at last.

"We are happy it pleases you." Ray smiled all humble-like.

"I shall have my men unload this and give you gas and food for the trip back North. Come—"

"Forgive us." Ray still smiled but his voice got a little different. "Our contract requires you pay us the money before you take possession of the Gold."

"A trifle," Don Escachza said grandly, "The money shall be sent to Laredo as agreed, and you personally shall be repaid for what you have done. Now, with your permission..."

Now mind, I was already upset about Samaniego keeping us fiddle-footing around here, and his give-a-damn attitude about paying for the Gold didn't help none neither. I couldn't exactly feel the pain in my finger anymore, but it was there at the back of my mind, making me nasty. And something about his choice of words bothered me: *you will be repaid for what you have done*—like he figured we had something coming we wasn't counting on.

"A moment," Ray spoke before I could, which was a good thing, and shifted so one hand hung down by his guns, "The contract requires payment here. And now."

"The contract," Don Escachza said smoothly, "is with *Mijnheer* Ryckman." He looked at us hard. "And where is he?"

Before Ray could answer he went on in a louder voice, "Ryckman is dead. This I know already. His widow and her father in Laredo, they know of his death also. But we do not yet know the facts of *Mijnheer* Ryckman's death—only that he died while in your company."

CHAPTER 33

Uh-oh.

"And now," Samaniego went on, like a judge handing down sentence. "You appear with the dead man's Gold and you wish me to pay you? Strangers?"

Now when I'm hurting and in a bad mood, I try not to discuss things too much. Especially not delicate matters like a dead man's Gold. This is because I realize in my wisdom that I'm not really at my best and most reasonable when I want to kill someone. So I just said,

"I feel myself losing my patience, Ray."

Way off in the distance I thought I heard something. Some fast-rumble sound. Gave it no notice. Don Escachza ignored it too and turned his eyes on me like the sights of a gun. "*Senor*, when you have reached my age, you will learn that patience is a precious thing to lose. But-" he lowered an eyebrow at me like it was a heavy club or something, the way you'd shake a stick. "-it is possible you may not reach my age."

"All right," I said it, but the words sounded like they came from someone else, plain and toneless. "Take a look at this."

I walked back over to the truck. My finger had quit hurting, or maybe I just didn't notice it in the heat of the kill-fever that was coming over me. I jumped in the back of the ambulance and climbed over the Gold, back to where we'd laid the German's body. Back there where nobody could see me real good, I picked up one of the shotguns, stuck it in the dead man's belt, and hand-hauled him out of there.

Smaniego's cowboys had been standing kind of close, but they backed way up fast when I came out the back of that ambulance pulling a corpse over across all that Gold. I dropped the body on the ground (face down, so nobody saw the scatter gun in his pants) and dragged it over to the wood pile close by the house, near to where our host was standing.

Don't know why I did this next thing. Don't know how I thought of it, or whether I was thinking at all. All I knew right then was I wanted to kill something, and I wanted it bad. Crazy bad. I pulled out the axe from the wood pile there and I chopped off the dead man's hand.

I guess everybody figured I'd gone loco, and maybe they were right. Anyway, they just stood clear still as I picked up that hand and tossed it on a table, right under the lamp light, where everyone could see the ring on the finger. That ring with the death-head and swastika.

"There's our credentials," I said.

And while they were all looking that way, I pulled the shotgun out of the dead man's belt and stepped right up to Samaniego, both barrels about half-a-foot from his belly.

"You listen to me." My voice sounded flat and far-off to me, like I was hearing someone read a phone book. Outside the courtyard, the deep-rumble sound had got closer and I could tell it was some kind of car or a truck maybe, coming in fast. But I paid it no mind.

"You will give us the money or I will go into your fine house and take it. If any of your men get in my way, I will kill them. And your family." I was getting mad enough to do it, too, looking forward to it in fact, and I couldn't figure out why my voice was so calm. "But first I will blast your insides clear across the yard. And if you doubt this, Don Escachza de Samaniego, you have only to try my patience."

I took a deep breath just to keep myself from shooting him too soon. "But remember," I said, "We killed to get that Gold. Killed many men. A few more such as you will make no difference."

Samaniego said nothing. Didn't move. Just looked at the shotgun, then over at the German's hand on his nice table, then back at the shotgun.

"We will have the money," Ray said, "One way or another," He had both his .45s out, his back to mine, covering Samaniego's men—who all seemed to have grown guns in their hands in the last half-minute.

I wonder if whoever wrote the words *Mexican stand-off* was there that night in the darkening, torch-lit courtyard of Don Escachza's hacienda, with all those bristling guns and men on the edge of using them. The rumbling sound—I could hear now it was a farm truck—had got close, then squealed to a stop, and we heard running boots but never took our eyes off each other.

"Listen to us Don Escachza," Ray said softly, his back still to the grandee, "I want no more killing. My soul is steeped in blood and I want no more. But if my friend fires that evil gun, there will not be enough left of you for your grandchildren to raise a marker over. Such a gun will tear you so much apart they will have to take down the wall behind you and bury the bricks, just to get a piece of you in the ground. And your men. And the others here. Their lives are in your keeping. Think of them and act wisely."

Samaniego's eyes never left mine. They might have wavered just a little, but they never looked down at the shotgun or over at the hand now. Just at me.

"I will not be robbed in my own house," he said.

"I never robbed anyone in my life," I lied, "and I won't start now if you bring out the money. Or back your men off, and we'll take the Gold someplace else and sell it. Or just stand there till I blast you into small pieces."

Off to one side, I could see that whoever had just drove up was in the courtyard now and he was trying to get the attention of one of the *caballeros* holding guns on us. Which was fine with me. If someone got distracted real good—give us time to start shooting first—me and Ray might just get past this.

"Ray," I said soft and in English, never taking my eyes off Samaniego, "that fellow over there..."

"I see him." Ray had been thinking along the same line as me. "If he gets enough attention this might work out for us."

"Well, Don Escachza?" I switched back to Spanish. "Is your mind made up to live or to die?"

"Go to the Devil."

"You first." I felt myself smiling, glad of what was coming and ready for it: Closing Time at Rancho Samaniego. "And when I catch up to you there, I'll kick your sorry hide all over Hell and back. See if I don't."

"Ray—" I switched back to English. "Looks like there's nothing else for it."

"I'm afraid not." I felt him tense up behind me. "You call it."

"I'm going to pivot," I said, "See how many of those cowboys I can put down with the scattergun. You do the same, we'll deal with Samaniego later."

"Sounds good to me."

"Ready?"

"Good luck, Culley."

"Good— wait- Let's see what the Hell this is..."

The new guy in the courtyard had convinced one of the *Caballeros* to let him get between them and our guns. It was a move dumb enough to draw respect, and it was also the excuse everyone had been looking for: No one lowered a gun, no one took their eyes off anyone else, but we all eased down a half-notch as the new guy tip-toed across the courtyard. And right up to Samaniego.

I don't know what the poor goof thought was going on here when he drove up, but he seemed to think whatever news he had was more important.

"*Patron?*" he squeaked, "I must say a word to you..."

Samaniego smiled. I'll give him credit, he smiled at a time like that, and said, "Must you, Bernardo? I do not look busy?"

"Much important," Bernardo insisted.

Samaniego raised an eyebrow at me, "Well, *Senor?*"

I backed the shotgun a few inches and nodded. Figured I didn't have to tell him not to move too far or too fast.

Bernardo took three careful steps over to Samaniego and started whispering frantically in his ear. Now and again the little guy pointed at me or Ray. Samaniego looked from us to the truck. And to the hand on his table. Then back to me again. And then the tension just drained away from his body. He raised his hands. Slow.

"*Muchachos,*" he called to his men, "put away your guns. Put them away now. Do this thing. These are my orders. Fetch the strong boxes. These men are my honored guests and they must not be harmed."

CHAPTER 34

L ike I say, I'd been sort of looking forward to killing somebody right then, but under the circumstances, I wasn't real disappointed to pass up this chance. The cowboys in the courtyard lost their guns as quick as they'd grew them, I lowered the shotgun and Ray holstered his .45s.

Next came the damnedest thing: Samaniego didn't exactly throw a party for us, but all at once me and Ray were quality folk around those parts. Someone took the dead hand off the table, and the women of the house brought out more liquor and some sweet chicken and honey cakes. They lighted up more torches all around, and right away two little boys came out toting generous-sized strong-boxes and set them on the table, along with two empty carpet-bags, big and sturdy-looking.

"You will wish to count it, Gentlemen." He opened one of the strong boxes, and everyone at the table kind of took a breath when they saw it was full of Yankee dollars, "Or shall I count it in your presence? That is better."

Ray and I ate while he counted out the money in front of us. Neither of us worried now.

Like I said before, these Spanish *Grandees* have pretty fixed ideas of hospitality. Once you're an honored guest, they'll feed you, keep you, protect you, and marry off their daughters to you as long as you're under their roof. It's like a sacred trust or something. Of course, when you get back on the road again, the wind from those parts can change awful sudden, but for now we were the fair-haired boys.

Don Escachza counted out the money, and it came to two hundred thousand dollars, which was considerable more than old Shlomo Rosenstern's people could have got for it on the black market up north, and maybe twice what it would have fetched legally in the States— if they could have sold it legal.

Two Hundred Thousand.

But you know, it's funny. The sight of all that nice green money stacked up on that table just didn't seem like so much, compared to the big pile of Gold glistening in the back of the ambulance.

Half a ton of shiny yellow Gold, and here we were trading it for bags of old dirty money.

Damn.

I snapped out of that pretty quick, I can tell you. Ray and I nodded while the boys stuffed piles of greenbacks neatly in the carpet bags, and we told our gracious host it was a pleasure doing business with him.

"Now," Don Escachza said formally, "we may unload the Gold from your truck. But it would be better, Senores, if you did not depart from here in that vehicle."

We looked curious about that and he turned to the nervous-looking guy who'd rode in and saved everybody a lot of grief.

"Tell them, Bernardo," Don Escachza raised his voice so everyone could hear, "Tell the story to us all!"

"Word reaches me," Bernardo pitched his voice like he was making a speech at a testimonial dinner or something. "Word reaches me of a massacre at a place called Old Pesos."

The crowd got quiet.

"Four days ago," he went on, "twelve fine men—strong, fine men—ride out from the town of Quenada. Three days later, only one rides back, and he brings with him the bodies of eleven others. This one man alone rides back, and the horses behind him carrying the bodies of his friends, the men of Quenada!

"The good people of the village, they drop to their knees to see such a sight. Old men weep openly, the women cry out, What could have happened?"

This Bernardo guy could see he had his crowd hooked real good, and he paused for effect before he went on. I was getting kind of interested myself to see how things turned out, and listened while he spun his yarn:

"The one who rode back, he is called Otilio, and his story is confused in some part but nonetheless impressive. Twenty men dead, he says—and these two left alive!"

An appreciative noise went through the crowd and Bernardo swept his arm to include me and Ray in the story, which was generous of him.

"Among the dead are the Serrano Brothers, all three, and their followers. Very bad men."

Another dramatic pause. More awe from the crowd. Then:

"They tried to take the Gold of Don Escachza de Soto de Sotomayor Samaniego!"

A murmur went across the table while everyone showed they were impressed as shucks about how bad the Serrano Brothers were, and Bernardo went on:

"And a lawman called Milianos, by all accounts a very dangerous man. He would take the Gold of Don Escachza, and now he lies dead," he continued in deep tones, "Also, alas, ten other fine men from the town of Quenada. Fine men, they say, but men who meant to take this Gold." He gestured at Ray's ambulance. "All dead. Twenty men dead and these two left alive. Twenty men died so that these two bloody men from Old Pesos might bring this Gold to our patron, Don Escachza de Soto de Sotomayor Samaniego!"

Sitting at the head of the table, with Ray and me on either side of him, Don Escachza beamed modestly.

And now I saw why the change in reception, why we were all of a sudden honored guests.

That scrape at Old Pesos was going to be a real folk tale in these parts—at least if Samaniego had anything to do with it. And he meant to bask in the glory. Hell, if he had his way, they'd be telling how we killed twenty men, then drove up to his place all bloody in a truck full of Gold with a dead man's hand, and sat down to dinner with him. They'd tell that story in the bunkhouse and in front of the fire for years to come. And they'd say the name of Don Escachza de Samaniego in a respectful whisper.

Don Escachza got Bernardo to tell the story a couple more times, and by the time he got finished, he had it to where Ray was charging up the hill on horseback with two Winchesters blazing in each hand, while I killed 'Cento Serrano in a bloody knife fight. And I tell you it made for good listening. I almost wished he'd get to the part about us burying the German on his motorcycle back there in the desert.

When it was all done, Samaniego nudged Bernardo, who said to us in a low voice, "A description of this fine vehicle of yours may have reached already the wrong ears. Perhaps it is better now if you do not leave the Rancho Samaniego in this truck you drove in."

Naturally, Don Escachza didn't want us picked up by *Federales*, *Rurales*, or anyone else. Better for the story if we just brought him his Gold and slipped away into legend and the desert.

Bernardo said, "Please permit me to buy it from you and allow me to give to you the truck in which I came: not a thing of beauty, but it will take you where you go."

And it wasn't no thing of beauty, neither. A cut-down farmer's truck, with big tires for bouncing across the cornfield when it had to, and looked old enough that God might have used it when He drove Adam and Eve from the Garden if He couldn't get anything nicer back then. But the engine ran honey-smooth.

When it was time to go, Bernardo gave Ray a few hundred *Pesos* and drove off in his ambulance while Samaniego escorted us over to our new transportation. Two little boys ran ahead, lugging our guns and the bags full of money, and Don Escachza walked grandly between us, almost arm-in-arm, and said in a low voice,

"A final thing, gentlemen. And note that I tell you this now, when I have no cause to lie:

"Our contract does indeed require that I pay you on receiving the Gold, which is the property of *Herr* Shlomo Rosenstern and his people, so that you may take it north to them in Texas. Earlier, when I refused to pay you this money; you must not think I intended to rob *Herr* Rosenstern or cheat him of any part of the money which he is promised. He is of my people, and I will not steal from my own. Don Escachza de Soto de Sotomayor Samaniego will not steal from his people. Not now, when so many depend upon it."

"You were worried," Ray said, "that we were just going to take the money and keep it?"

The old guy looked awkward. For some reason I piped up, "Now what makes you think we won't?"

"So many depend upon this money." Samaniego watched a little sadly as the boys stowed the bags and guns behind the old canvas seats in the farm truck, and he sighed, kind of. "*Herr* Rosenstern wrote me of it. Families follow him from the old world, a thousand, maybe more, all with their futures bound up together by this money. And they are of my people. Perhaps you will take it from them, rob them of all this." He gave me a look. "Such a thing is possible. But that is between you and your God—whatever that may be..."

I got the impression he figured any God that'd have me in His church couldn't be much.

Then he went on in a whole different tone:

"But I would rather tell this tale to my grandchildren than be remembered in the story as another who fell before the guns of the bloody men from Old Pesos."

CHAPTER 35

I'd drove about a mile down the road when Ray turned to me and asked, "What he said back there about his people: does that mean he's Jewish?"

"Said he was. And like he also said, no reason to lie about it." I settled back in the seat. "I read in college one time how a lot of Jews came over from Spain to get away from the Inquisition, years back. I guess back then if you made the trip over here and grabbed enough land, killed enough Indians, and just generally acted Catholic, nobody looked at your background too close. The way this book said it, there's secret Jews all over Mexico."

"It makes sense I guess," Ray nodded, "And when I think of it, did you notice he didn't come out and do business with us till after sunset?"

"Yeah?"

"I just remembered, today's Saturday. That's a Jewish thing, isn't it?"

"Damned if I know. But by the way, Ray, you were right. About letting Otilio go, back to 'Nada. Probably saved our lives."

"You think so?"

"I been studying on it," I said, "And the way I see it, Samaniego must have a man in Quenada. That would be that Bernardo fella. I think I seen him at the bar the night we showed up. Hell, Samaniego's probably got connections all over these parts, and when you and Ryckman didn't turn up with the Gold, every one of them put an ear to the ground."

We came to a grade in the road and I went through the gears, getting the feel of the farm truck, and learning not to push it too hard or too sharp.

"What I'm thinking is," I went on, "a few days ago back when we blew into 'Nada, this Bernardo got word to Samaniego and told him Ryckman was dead—Samaniego said he knew about that, remember. But it wasn't till tonight Bernardo told him about the fight at Old Pesos. And he wouldn't have heard about it at all if Stable-Boy hadn't got back to 'Nada and told about it. Which he never would have done if you hadn't stopped me from killing him back there at Old Pesos."

"What are you saying exactly?" Ray yawned like it was hard for him to keep up with all this.

"I'm just saying you were right, that's all. It was smart of you not to let me kill Otilio."

"Smart's got nothing to do with it," Ray sighed, "It was just the right thing to do; you shouldn't go killing a man if you don't have to."

"Maybe that's so. I'm just saying maybe it was the right thing and the smart thing both."

"I told you, life is funny sometimes."

"And you were right about that too."

Some little time passed, and then I said, "We heading straight back to Laredo? And Ryckman's widow?"

"Unless you need to stop for candy on the way," he yawned, "Do you mind driving the first stretch?"

"No, go ahead and get some sleep."

We still had a few hours till daylight as I headed the old farm truck north up the highway toward Laredo, which we would hit about this time tomorrow.

Just me, Ray, and all that money.

And Ray asleep.

I pressed gently on the gas pedal. The Harrington shifted a little on my left hip and hung in easy reach off the edge of the seat. Now and then the holster swayed with the motion of the truck, reminding me it was there.

Seamus Feeney would have said it was time to set my priorities.

CHAPTER 36

Not much to tell after that. We headed north, slipped across the border near Laredo, and gave the money to Ryckman's widow.

Along the way, we sold most of the firearms to a gunsmith at a little place just south of the crossing. We thought about maybe just pitching them in the river since we didn't want to be showing those guns around Mexico just then, but Ray worried about carrying them that close to the border, and if anyone spotted us tossing them away, well, that'd just naturally look kind of guilty. So we sold them for what we could get, which wasn't much, and used it for our travel expenses. Together with what Ray got for his truck, and the money I'd picked up back at old Pesos and off the dead German, it made a tidy sum enough, I guess.

Ray kept the .45s; said they belonged to the Army, and he meant to go back there. I bought a box of cigars (I was getting a taste for them.) put them in a paper bag, and stowed the Harrington in the cigar box.

Funny, it felt real good not to wear a gun anymore. Like someone had been standing on my foot and finally got off it.

Once we got into Laredo we managed to get cleaned up and dressed up—since the Depression, you could buy second-hand clothes pretty cheap, and good ones, too—and I covered the shotgun shell on my short finger with a clean white bandage so we didn't look so much like the Bloody Men from Old Pesos before we called on Rebecca Ryckman at a nice apartment there in town.

Recognized her soon as she opened the door, from the picture in Ryckman's wallet. It was a nice picture, but it didn't do her justice. She wasn't beautiful like the women in magazine pictures, and I don't know if I can tell it, but just some look in her eyes, the sound her voice had, the way she looked at you when you talked, made you want to spend time with her. Also, her belly was round and swollen out like a big ball, and—I don't know, I guess she had that look some women get when they've got a baby coming and feel blessed by it.

And when he saw that belly, Ray kind of glanced quick at me, like he'd figured out now why Ryckman's woman hadn't made the trip with him.

That woman, the look on her face when we talked, it reminded me of how another woman used to look at me like that, years back. I'm not saying I'd give up my religion for her if I had any. Or die in the desert just to make her proud of me, nothing like that. But I could see Ryckman's point of view on the subject.

We told her who we were, and we said how Ryckman died saving both our lives, and while we talked about him she just sat there with that look on her face, and her eyes turning red and blinking back tears. We waited a minute and then we set the bags of money on her living room carpet and opened them up for her.

I've never seen anyone look at money like she did. Big money, folks see that much in one place, they usually get a funny look on their face, and it ain't pretty—I get that look myself, so I know. But when she looked down at it, all it meant to her was that her man had lived up to his promise and now she could take this back to her dad and her people, and hold her head up around them.

What Milianos said to Otilio back there in the desert come back to me: about having something in your life to look back on and be proud of. She had that now.

"You must take some for your trouble," she said when she could talk again, "Please. Whatever..."

Ray reached for one of the bags and pulled it over to him.

"*Mijnheer* Ryckman promised me fifty dollars for this work, Madam," he took out two twenties and a ten, "we are settled now."

"And you?" She looked at me.

Ray looked at me.

"Hel-heck, I was coming this way anyhow," I said, "Just glad for the ride."

CHAPTER 37

So I guess that's what I got out of my whole seven years at Old Pesos: just about what I went down with, plus that look on the widow Ryckman's face to think back on. What the Mexicans call *nada*.

I tried not to feel too bad about it. Guess I've done stupider things in my day. None come to mind off-hand though.

Ray, as we walked out onto the street a ways, he said, "And for my pains, she gave me a world of sighs."

"Whuzza?"

"Just something I read once. Seems like a long time ago. It's from OTHELLO."

"Took me a minute, but I remember it now. Ain't that the story you told that girl at the Palacio? The night all your trouble started?"

"I guess so," Ray got a thoughtful look on that ugly face of his. "Or maybe what looks like trouble sometimes is just another door opening up, taking you somewhere you didn't think of going."

Maybe so, but you would have had a hard time selling me that notion back when I was lying on the floor of that stinking cell in 'Nada, looking up at the bottom of Otilio's hob-nailed boot. Or out at Old Pesos, staring wide-eyed down the barrel of Tony Serrano's rifle. But I just said,

"Or maybe you should buy me a drink."

Laredo was a toney town back then, and when we left the widow, Ray and I got a pretty good meal at a nice restaurant. Then we walked towards the train depot, so's I could find out about getting back to Kansas City. Didn't know what Ray planned, but I kind of figured he'd go back to the Army. The depot at Laredo was a fine big old building in those days, and when we got there, it happened there was a train out to Kansas City around Midnight. I bought me a ticket.

"How about you?" I asked, "Ain't you heading back to the Army?"

"Not anymore." Ray looked thoughtful. "I've been thinking I'll stay around Laredo some. Maybe meet old man Rosenstern and see if he's hiring any help these days."

"Reckon he needs a truck driver?"

"Could be," he nodded, "If not, I'll find something else. The way I see it, Mrs. Ryckman's going to need someone around for a while, and-and I guess I'll just stop here a while. What about you? Want to stick around?"

"No offense to you and this fine city, Ray, but I figured I'd get back to Kansas City and ask around about that girl I used to know. Decide what to do about her, if I still got the chance."

Then we just stood there in the depot, feeling kind of awkward I guess, I could see across the street there was a nice-looking saloon: the kind of place where they serve cool, sweet drinks at a shiny bar, where the boy calls you "sir" and women across the room notice your nice clothes and smile for you. And I had near a hundred dollars in my pocket.

"I guess before I get going." I nudged Ray and we headed across the street. "I'll have a drink, smoke a cigar, maybe spend some time."

"Sounds like a fine plan." Ray smiled. "Wish I could do that myself, but I better find a room for the night. And start thinking to save my money. I might need to get a new truck or something. Have a drink for me, eh?"

"I'll have a couple. For you."

We'd got to the saloon door now, and Ray said, "By the way, Thanks."

"Thanks for what?"

"For not killing me back there. *Gracias.*"

I wondered if he knew, if he even suspected just then, how close I come to doing that.

But I just answered, "*De nada.*"

"I mean it," he insisted, "The way *Mijnheer* Ryckman and I came sailing in out of no place like that, bringing all our trouble with us... You didn't know us, you didn't owe us anything but grief. Hell, I wouldn't have blamed you if you just shot us and took all you could carry."

Yeah, I wouldn't have blamed me much either. Too late for that now, though. But I wondered something:

"Come to that, Ray, what made you trust me? How'd you know I wasn't going to just kill you in your sleep and make off with whatever?"

He looked at me like I just asked a dumb question.

"Your bookshelves," he said.

"Beg pardon?"

"Your bookshelves." Like he was repeating a lesson for a slow child. "I looked at them when we first arrived. And I knew right then, a man who'd read books like you had, books like those – well, I just knew I could trust a man like you. That's all."

"That's all?"

Just shows how wrong a man can be, even an educated man like Ray, thinking he could trust me, not knowing how near I come to making myself rich over his dead body. And right now, I couldn't remember why I hadn't done just that. I was going to have to think on it, and on what he said, think on it long and deep, and the inside of this saloon might be the right place to start.

"If you get back this way." Ray turned to go. "Come and look me up. When you get a chance."

"I'll do that," I said.

But I guess I never got around to it.

THE END

AUTHOR BIO

Daniel Boyd is a retired police officer, old-movie buff, and HAMLET scholar who makes tobacco pipes in his spare time.